A sweet ache urged Holly to lean into Gray and return his kiss.

But, to her dismay, Gray pulled away from her.

'Holly.'

Noooo. She kept her eyes tightly closed.

In the stillness she could hear the hammering of her heartbeat and the reckless pace of Gray's breathing. He dropped a soft kiss on the bridge of her nose, then moved further away.

'What—?' she began, then had to pause to catch her breath.

His sexy blue eyes were apologetic. 'I'm sorry,' he said.

Sorry? How could he share the hottest kiss of her life, and then apologise as if it were a mistake?

Distraught, Holly stared at him. 'Why are you sorry?'

'I shouldn't have done that.' His throat rippled as he swallowed. 'Please don't read too much into it.'

What a klutz she was. She'd gone into swoon mode, allowing herself to be completely carried away, while Gray had merely found a new technique to stop her from asking questions. *Damn Gray.* She could still feel the warm pressure of his lips on hers. She could still smell him and taste him. Could still feel the ripples of pleasure pooling inside her like aftershocks.

But for Gray the kiss had been a game, a purely practical ploy to stop yet another conversation.

RANCHER'S TWINS: MUM NEEDED

BY
BARBARA HANNAY

First published in Great Britain 2011
by Mills & Boon, an imprint of Harlequin (UK) Limited,
Eton House, 18-24 Paradise Road, Richmond, Surrey TW9 1SR

© Barbara Hannay 2011

ISBN: 978 0 263 22012 4

Harlequin (UK) policy is to use papers that are natural, renewable and recyclable products and made from wood grown in sustainable forests. The logging and manufacturing process conform to the legal environmental regulations of the country of origin.

Printed and bound in Great Britain
by CPI Antony Rowe, Chippenham, Wiltshire

Barbara Hannay was born in Sydney, educated in Brisbane, and has spent most of her adult life living in tropical North Queensland, where she and her husband have raised four children. While she has enjoyed many happy times camping and canoeing in the bush, she also delights in an urban lifestyle—chamber music, contemporary dance, movies and dining out. An English teacher, she has always loved writing, and now, by having her stories published, she is living her most cherished fantasy.

In 2007 Barbara won the RITA® Award for Best Traditional Romance with CLAIMING HIS FAMILY. ADOPTED: OUTBACK BABY was a 2009 RITA® Award finalist.

To catch up on all Barbara's latest news visit www.barbarahannay.com

I'd like to thank Anne Gracie,
for her wonderful insights into adult literacy,
and Elliot, my live-in bush poet.

CHAPTER ONE

THEY were asleep.

At last.

Holly held her breath as she closed the storybook, then backed out of the children's room with the stealth of a special ops soldier.

The caution was necessary. Really. These kids could sleep soundly through the familiar blast of car horns and sirens from the busy New York street below, but the tiniest squeak from within the apartment could rouse them to instant panicking wakefulness.

This evening, to Holly's relief, neither child stirred. They lay perfectly still in their matching bunk beds. In striped pyjamas, one dark head and one fair, they clutched their favourite fluffy toys—a kangaroo for Josh, a koala for Anna—and their eyes remained blessedly closed.

Holly reached the doorway without a mishap and quickly flicked the light switch, plunging the room into darkness. For once there were no responding squawks or protests. Just sweet, blissful silence.

She tiptoed down the hall…and the silence continued.

Fannnntastic. With a little luck, tonight would be a good night. No wet beds. No nightmares. In the past month there'd only been a handful of good nights. But, before

Holly could even think about letting out a sigh of relief, her cellphone rang.

No-o-o!

With the speed of a baseball short stop, she dived across the room, snatched the phone from the coffee table and darted into her bedroom, closing the door quickly but softly behind her.

The phone's screen identified the caller. Her boyfriend, Brandon. *Wonderful.*

'Hi, Brand,' she whispered.

No squeaks emanated from the bedroom down the hall and she sank gratefully onto the bed.

'Holly, why are you whispering?'

'I've just got the twins to sleep.'

'Oh, right.' Brandon gave an audible sigh. 'How are they coping this week?'

'A little better.'

'That's great.'

Great wasn't quite the word Holly would have chosen to describe the small improvement in the children's progress, but of course she wouldn't correct Brandon. He'd given her fabulous support during the funeral and its aftermath.

'I got your message,' he said.

'Right. Thanks for calling back.' Holly took a moment to relax into the pillows and she deliberately lightened her tone. 'So, what do you think? Can you wangle a leave pass for this weekend?'

She crossed her fingers as she waited for his answer. *Please come, Brand. I need you.*

Brandon's family owned a dairy farm in Vermont and his dad's health wasn't the best, so the responsibility of running the enterprise had fallen squarely on Brandon's shoulders.

So, yes—it was asking a lot to expect him to get away to New York again so soon. Last month, after Holly's cousin Chelsea's sudden and tragic death, he'd taken almost a whole week off to be with her and to help with the children.

That was pretty amazing, actually. Holly had been touched and surprised. Since she'd moved away from Vermont to study in New York, she'd come to accept that if she wanted to see her boyfriend it was up to her to make the effort. She'd grown up on a dairy farm, too, so she understood the demands and she'd been prepared to be the one who did all the travelling. Even so, she'd only been able to see Brandon a handful of times in this past year.

If he came this weekend, she would make sure they had time alone together. She and Brandon had been an item since high school, almost six years. Very soon now, she would be finished with her studies, Anna and Josh would be settled in Australia with their father, and she was looking forward to going home to Vermont to settle down with Brand.

She could so easily picture their lives together—Brandon with his dairy herd, while she worked in the local school, the two of them balancing their day jobs with their life at home, and eventually, with a family of their own—copper-haired children like their dad.

Holly was very happy with that picture, and thinking about her boyfriend always made her feel cosy and safe.

Admittedly, most girls might not place cosiness and safety high on their wish list when it came to boyfriends, but Holly wasn't looking for a guy who spelled excitement and passion. Her cousin Chelsea, the twins' mother, had taken that risk and the result had been divorce and heartbreak.

'I don't know if I can get away this weekend,' Brandon said suddenly.

Holly suppressed a sigh. 'I do understand, honey, but—'

'Do you?' His voice bristled with unexpected impatience. 'Because I *don't* understand why you're complicating this, Holly. The children's father is on his way at last, so why do you need me? Why do you need my help if he's going to be there, too?'

'It would just be good to have your support. I've looked after the twins for a month and now I have to say goodbye.'

Holly suppressed a sigh. She needed to be calm and composed when she talked with Gray about his children, and she would have liked a little backup from Brandon. She needed to explain to Gray about Anna and Josh's schooling needs, their eating habits, their fears…

The twins had been at home on the day Chelsea had collapsed, and it was six-year-old Josh who'd courageously dialled 911. They hadn't only lost their mommy; they'd suffered a terrible trauma. Anna's nightmares were truly terrifying.

Holly needed to explain all this to their estranged father, but it would be so much easier if her steady and reliable boyfriend was there as well. As a buffer. An anchor. A safety net.

'Actually, Holly, I can't come this weekend.'

The sudden nervousness in Brandon's voice penetrated the whirl of Holly's thoughts.

Why was he nervous? Brandon was never nervous. Was something wrong?

'There's…um…there's something I should tell you,' he said.

'What is it?'

'It's really hard to explain. I…I don't know how to say this, but…'

Holly's insides froze and she was gripped by a terrible deer-in-the-headlights fear.

Brandon cleared his throat.

She forced herself to ask, 'Brandon, what's the matter?'

'I didn't want to tell you before—because of Chelsea and everything…'

'Tell me what?' she almost screamed. He was scaring her.

Brandon cleared his throat again.

Holly gripped the phone tighter, squeezing her eyes to hold back threatening tears.

Was Brandon trying to break-up with her?

No. No. Surely not.

Like someone drowning, her mind flashed back through precious memories. The school dance when they'd first met. Brandon helping her with algebra homework at the big scrubbed table in her mother's cosy kitchen. The familiar, comfortable texture of his lips. The ruby heart locket he'd given her on Valentine's Day three years ago. The way she liked to bury her nose against the warm freckles on his neck when he held her. The cosy sense of safety that she'd always felt with him…

Now, suffocating panic filled her throat.

She couldn't bear to think about losing him, especially not when she'd just lost Chelsea. Fear pulled tight knots in her stomach.

Brandon said, 'You have to agree it's not really working for us.'

'What do you mean?' she bleated.

'We only see each other a few times a year.'

'But I've almost finished my studies.' Her voice was shrill now. Pleading. 'I'll soon be home for good and we can—'

'I'm so sorry, Holly. You see, the thing is...I...I've met someone else.'

CHAPTER TWO

As the taxi pulled into the kerb on West 69th Street Gray Kidman was thinking about the first time he'd arrived at this red-brick apartment block. He'd been a bridegroom then, fired with love and certainty and hope, with no premonition of the heartache that lay ahead of him.

This time he knew what he was in for, knew the challenges and the very real chances for failure. Right now, as he stepped onto the pavement and looked up to the level where his children were waiting, his stomach felt like a jar full of jumping grasshoppers.

His hand was actually shaking as he pressed the security buzzer.

The children answered immediately.

'Daddy!'

'Hi, Dad.'

Gray closed his eyes, momentarily stunned by the emotion his children's voices aroused. For three long months he'd been waiting for this. First, the wet season floods had held him up, then a broken ankle after a desperate attempt to cross a raging creek. Now, at last, he dipped his head to the speaker phone. 'G'day, scallywags.'

Anna squealed, 'I'll press the button to let you in.'

'I've already pressed it,' shouted Josh, full of self-importance and equally excited.

A wry smile tilted Gray's mouth and the glass doors slid open, allowing him access to the apartment block's foyer. He hefted his duffel bag over one shoulder and strode with only the slightest hint of a limp across the blue-tiled floor. As he pressed the lift button, he reminded himself that he must remember to call this an elevator now. His kids would be quick to correct him.

His kids…

His stomach jumped like crazy.

Taking sole charge of Anna and Josh was a huge task, probably the toughest challenge he'd ever faced. He wanted the very best for them. If it was in his power, he'd give his children the perfect foundation for their lives—a safe and comfortable home, a loving family network, and the best possible education.

The irony was that they had all of the above right here in New York City. This apartment block was secure and modern. His ex-wife's teacher cousin was a first-rate nanny, and the children's doting grandparents were nearby. The school they attended had won all kinds of awards for educational excellence.

Although it had nearly killed Gray to let his wife walk away from his Outback cattle property, taking their children with her, he'd been forced to accept that Anna and Josh were better off here in New York than in his home in one of the remotest corners of Australia.

He hadn't given in without a fight but, despite his heartbreak, he'd eventually let his family go.

Yet, tragically, here he was, reclaiming his children and taking them halfway across the world to the very situation their mother had fled from.

Gray had no other option. Running a cattle station was his only income-earning skill. Jabiru Creek Station was the best he had to offer. It was all he had to offer.

He was very afraid it wasn't enough.

The elevator arrived and shot him quickly to the third floor, and when the doors slid open his children were waiting for him.

'Daddy!' Anna launched herself, like a small torpedo, straight into Gray's arms.

He let his duffel bag slip to the floor and lifted her high and she clasped him tightly around his neck.

'Daddy! My daddy!' She buried her face into his shoulder and her silky fair hair smelled wonderfully of flowers.

'Hey, Dad.' Josh was standing close, looking up expectantly.

Crouching, Gray juggled Anna onto one knee and hugged his son. What a fine little fellow Josh was. Gray had been moved to tears when he'd heard that his small son had been brave and quick-thinking when his mother collapsed at home, rushing to dial Emergency.

Now...how good it was to embrace them both. At last.

They seemed fine. Gray had been worried he'd find them pale and pining, but they looked happy and healthy and bursting with energy. It was such a relief.

'That's some welcome,' a voice said and he looked up to see a young woman with dark hair and dark shiny eyes standing in the apartment's open doorway.

Holly O'Mara, Chelsea's young cousin. Gray sent her a smile that felt crooked with emotion. He winced at the twinge in his ankle when he stood once more.

'Holly,' he said, holding out his hand.

'It's good to see you, Gray.'

He didn't know this young woman very well. On the rare occasions they'd met at family gatherings, Holly had always been shy, keeping well in the background, as if she preferred her own company, so he'd never gone out of his way to chat with her. Besides, she was training to be an English teacher, which meant she was as well educated and cultured as his former wife, another woman destined to remind him of his inadequacies.

But he couldn't deny he owed her a great deal. She'd been sole carer of his children for three long, difficult months.

With the twins skipping at his heels, he followed Holly inside the apartment. It was then, without warning, that he was sideswiped by a new emotion—the realisation that his beautiful bride was gone for ever.

It was crazy to feel like this now. Truth was, Gray had already lost Chelsea three years ago when she left him. He'd done his grieving then, and in time he'd moved on, eventually finding comfort in a healthy cynicism for the married state.

Now, suddenly, the finality of her passing hit him like a physical blow. A sense of loss descended like black, suffocating cloud.

Don't break down. Not now. Not in front of the children.

He heard Holly say gently, 'You've had a long journey. Why don't you go through to the living room? Take the weight off. I have coffee brewing.'

Gray was grateful for the normality and everyday ease of her welcome. 'Thanks,' he said. 'Thanks for everything, Holly.'

Their gazes met in an unexpected moment of connection. Holly was smiling, but Gray thought he saw tears glistening in her dark eyes and he felt a painful tightening in his throat.

He spoke more gruffly than he meant to. 'Come on, kids, show me the way.'

* * *

Holly told herself to keep smiling as she watched Gray and his children head down the hall. Alone in the kitchen, however, she was fighting tears as she filled the coffee-maker.

It was two months now since her break-up with Brandon, but Gray's arrival *at last* brought it all back—memories of the horrible phone call, the heartbreak in the following weeks of anxiety, of hoping against all hope for another call. *It was all a mistake, Holly. I really do love you.*

But on top of that pain...she felt so tense, so conflicted about this reunion.

Oh, she was very happy for Anna and Josh. She knew how much they needed their father, and it was wonderful to see how thrilled they were. But she wasn't sure she could bear to let them go all the way back to Australia.

Of course, Gray had every right to take his children home, and there was no denying that he loved them.

Just now, when he'd hunkered down in the corridor to hug them, Holly had seen the way he closed his eyes and held them close against his heart. She'd watched the concentrated emotion in his face, and she'd been so moved she'd almost spoiled the moment by weeping.

Until then, she hadn't realised how fragile she was after the emotional pressure cooker of the last three months.

She and the children had been through so much together, and they'd grown incredibly close. When Chelsea had died so suddenly, the very foundations of their world had been shaken and Holly had needed to dig deep, discovering a sensitivity and wisdom she hadn't known she possessed.

Even though Chelsea's parents lived close by in a luxury Westside apartment, they'd been too shocked and grieving to be of much help. They'd gladly handed over their grandchildren into Holly's full-time care until Gray Kidman arrived to claim them.

Looking back, Holly wasn't quite sure how she'd managed. In a cruelly short space of time she'd lost Chelsea, her cousin and her best friend, and then Brandon. Filled with despair, she'd wanted to crawl away and hide for a decade or two, and she might have done exactly that if Anna and Josh's needs hadn't been even greater than hers.

To give them the love and attention they'd needed, she'd been forced to put her own heartbreak aside.

So…in a way the children had saved her. But right now, she was finding it hard to accept that her role as an integral player in this little team was almost over. She couldn't imagine living without them.

'Look, Daddy.' Anna lifted her top lip.

'Wow. You've lost a tooth.'

The little girl grinned proudly, revealing the gap. 'I left it under my pillow and the Tooth Fairy came.'

'Lucky you.'

'Josh hasn't lost any teeth yet.'

His son's lips were tightly pressed together, and Gray caught a flicker of embarrassment in the boy's eyes. Clearly, sibling rivalry was alive and well, and no doubt Josh felt left behind in the race to shed baby teeth.

'Josh must have extra tough teeth,' Gray suggested.

The boy sent him a grateful smile.

To change the subject, Gray unzipped a pocket on the outside of his duffel bag and drew out a small packet.

'Is that a present?' asked Anna, eager-eyed.

'It's a game to share with your brother. A card game. Snap. With pictures of the Outback on the back.'

'Your Outback?'

He smiled uncertainly. 'Yes. My Outback.'

The twins had been three when they'd left his home—he doubted they'd remember it.

They knelt at the coffee table as Gray fanned the cards onto its smooth glass surface, showing bright photos of kangaroos, pink-flowering gum trees and wide red plains shimmering beneath sunburned skies.

'Is that where you're going to take us?' asked Josh.

Gray nodded.

'Is your house like this one?' Anna picked up a card that showed a faded, shabby homestead with a broad iron roof standing alone in the middle of a sparse red desert.

'More or less,' Gray admitted with some reluctance.

The little girl stared with large worried eyes at the rather ugly house and stark forbidding landscape.

'We have more trees than that and quite a decent garden,' Gray amended, feeling rather like a real estate agent trying to sell inadequate property. 'My homestead is painted white, and there are lots of extra buildings.'

'What kind of buildings?'

He realised now that he should have brought proper photos of Jabiru Creek Station, instead of these generic tourist images. 'We have machinery sheds and storage sheds and houses for the ringers.'

'What are ringers?'

'They're stockmen.'

'Cowboys,' added Holly cheerfully as she came into the room with a coffee pot and two black and white mugs.

'Except that in Australia we don't call them cowboys,' Gray amended with a smile.

'Can we ride horses?'

The animated excitement in Josh's face was a stark contrast to the sudden fear in Anna's dark brown eyes. Gray's chest tightened. His daughter looked so much like her mother. So beautiful, like a delicate flower, and right now, so worried and sad.

'I have a nice little horse that you can learn to ride,' he

told Josh. For Anna's sake he added, 'But you don't have to ride if you don't want to.'

He tried to cheer Anna with a smiling wink. She wouldn't remember how she used to love to ride in the saddle in front of him, while he kept one arm around her and one hand holding the reins. To his dismay, her lower lip trembled. Damn. He had so little experience in handling kids. The simplest thing could suddenly become a huge problem.

Holly, who'd made herself comfortable in an armchair, leaned forward and picked up another card—a picture of blue sky reflected in a large pool of water at the bottom of a steep red-walled gorge.

'Look, Anna,' Holly said. 'Isn't this beautiful?'

Over the children's heads, her expressive dark eyes sent Gray a silent message. They needed to change the subject.

'Do you have beautiful places like this on your ranch?' she asked him.

'Sure. We have a fabulous deep gorge and a sizeable river.'

'Can you swim there?' Holly asked with an encouraging smile.

Not unless you're willing to risk being eaten by a crocodile.

Sidestepping that question, Gray said instead, 'There's a dam near the homestead where you can swim.' *When it's not too hot or muddy.*

He tentatively touched his daughter's arm. Her skin was soft and smooth and perfect and his heart lurched. He hated to think of her being muddy or sunburned or in any kind of danger from the harsh environment that was his home.

Would he be able to take proper care of her? He hunted for something positive to tell her.

'Do you like puppies, Anna?'

She nodded solemnly.

'I have a nice kelpie and she's going to have babies very soon. By the time we get home there might be puppies.'

'How many puppies?'

'Maybe three or four.'

Anna's eyes widened. 'Are they all in their mommy's tummy?'

'Yes. They're growing fat and wriggly and they're almost ready to be born.'

'Like Josh and me? We were together in our mommy's tummy.'

Gray tensed, expecting his daughter to burst into tears now that she'd inadvertently mentioned her mother. His skin grew clammy. His heart picked up pace. Hell. What should he do and say now?

Holly spoke for him. 'That's right, Anna. The puppies are just like you and Josh, all together in their mommy's tummy.' She said this smoothly and calmly, as if nothing awkward or dangerous had happened. 'If there are three puppies, they'll be triplets. If there are four they'll be quads.'

To Gray's surprise, Anna grinned, clearly pleased with Holly's answer.

'Why don't you two have a game of Snap while your dad drinks his coffee?' Holly suggested next. 'Take the cards through to your room. I'll call you as soon as lunch is ready.'

'Is Dad having lunch with us?' Josh asked.

'Of course. He'll be staying here with us for a few days.'

Satisfied, the boy began to gather up the cards and the two trotted happily off to their room.

As they left, Gray sent Holly a surprised smile, shaking

his head. 'They did exactly what you asked. Are they always so obedient?'

She laughed. 'Heavens, no. Although they're getting better all the time.' She poured coffee into two mugs. 'Here's your coffee. Drink it while it's hot.'

'Thanks.' He relaxed into the sofa and took a deep sip. The coffee was indeed hot and strong and of very good quality.

Over the rim of his mug he stole a closer look at Holly O'Mara. Although he'd only met her a few times, he was sure there was something different about her. He tried to decide what it was. Was her face thinner? Was that why her dark eyes now looked larger, her mouth more curving and lush, her cheekbones more defined?

Or was there something different about her expression?

The change was hard to pin down, but he sensed a depth in Chelsea's young cousin that he'd never been aware of before. He knew these past three months must have been very hard on her. No doubt she'd had to grow up fast.

Whatever it was about Holly that was different, the change seemed to suit her. *And* she'd clearly done a very good job of looking after his children.

'I hope you realise how very grateful I am,' he said. 'Honestly, the way you've taken care of the twins has been amazing. Fantastic. It can't have been easy—being dumped with everything after…after Chelsea…'

Holly nodded. 'There have been some grim moments, but each day gets better.'

Gray wondered, somewhat anxiously, about the 'grim moments'. He sat for a bit in silence, wrapped in worried thoughts as they drank their coffee.

'How's your ankle?' Holly asked politely.

'Oh, it's fine.' He pulled a face, remembering the

exasperation of the floods, and then the further frustration of his accident. 'You have no idea how maddening it
was not being able to get here any sooner.'

She let out a soft huff. 'I'll admit it wasn't easy at this
end, either, trying to convince Anna and Josh that you were
held up all that time by floods.'

'I'm sorry.'

She shook her head. 'No, you couldn't help it, and you
did the right thing when you asked me not to tell them
about the accident. They'd just lost their mom. They would
have been devastated if they'd heard their dad was hurt,
too.'

'I wouldn't have been much use to them on crutches.'

'Imagine your journey home,' Holly agreed, smiling.
'Twenty-something hours on a plane and trying to manage
six-year-old twins while you're hobbling on a cast.'

'Exactly.' Gray sat forward, eager to voice the question that had been plaguing him. 'So—how do you think
Anna and Josh will cope with going back to Australia with
me?'

He hoped she would answer with an easygoing shrug
and a quick reassurance.

They'll be fine. They're over the worst now.

To his dismay, she dropped her gaze to her coffee cup
and twisted it in her hands.

His throat tightened uncomfortably. 'I thought my
place—somewhere completely different—might help them.
Might be a…a distraction.'

Holly looked up again and, when her dark eyes met his,
she was frowning. He saw no hint of reassurance.

He spoke again quickly, needing to strengthen his case.
'This apartment must hold so many sad memories for the
children. Won't it help them to get away?'

Her mouth opened again as if she was going to reply, but then she hesitated.

Gray's entire body tensed. 'You agree, don't you?' He forced an awkward shrug. 'I admit you know my children better than I do. I'd value your opinion.'

She responded with a faint smile. 'I certainly hope they'll be fine, but I can't promise it's going to be easy, Gray. I'm no expert, but from everything I've read—'

'Everything you've *read?*' He felt himself tense. As a cattleman who'd always relied on purely practical skills, he was sceptical about the glorified merits of the written word.

Perhaps Holly sensed his doubt. Her cheeks flushed deep pink but, when she spoke, she lifted her chin and her dark eyes narrowed. 'I've never had any first-hand experience of grief, certainly not with helping children who've lost a parent. So I consulted a GP who referred me to a psychologist, and I've done some reading, too. After all, the books are written by experts.'

The skin on the back of Gray's neck grew hot. Not quite meeting her gaze, he said, 'So what did the experts have to say?'

Holly set her coffee mug on the table with exquisite care, as if it were a rare antique. 'It seems that children who've suffered a loss can benefit from a predictable routine and structure. The familiarity of a routine helps them to feel secure.'

A predictable routine.

Structure.

Security.

Gray's heart sank. Predictability and security were scarce commodities in the Outback. Cattlemen and their families lived at the mercy of the elements, or at the whim of fluctuating markets. Daily, they dealt with the problems caused by isolation and vast distances.

He recalled all the things his ex-wife had hated about his lifestyle, and he thought about his experience over the past three months—being cut off by the floods, almost running out of supplies, busting his leg in a flooded river.

Doubts crowded in. What was he doing here? How could he take his kids away from this safe and secure world that they knew and loved?

Abruptly, he stood and strode to the window where he dipped a slat in the blinds with one finger and stared down at the crowded pavements and busy traffic below.

Without looking at Holly, he said grimly, 'If the experts in your books are right, the last thing my children need is another big change.'

Unhappily, he folded his arms over his chest and his jaw jutted belligerently. 'I'm planning to drag Anna and Josh halfway across the world to a place that's completely different from here, and your book-writing experts are telling me it's the worst thing I can do.'

CHAPTER THREE

For a moment, Holly was seriously tempted to tell Gray that yes, his children would be much better off if they stayed right here in Manhattan. Of course they'd be happier if they were allowed to continue in this familiar environment—living in this apartment, going to their highly acclaimed school, playing with their select circle of appropriate friends.

For three months she'd been trying to follow the psychologists' advice. She'd built little rituals into the children's days so they always had something to look forward to.

She'd carefully planned mealtimes around their favourite nutritious foods, and she'd scheduled regular after school treats. Of course, she'd made sure that bedtime was special with their favourite stories. And plenty of hugs.

But she couldn't suggest that Gray would not be able to meet his children's needs. She'd witnessed his deep emotion when he'd first greeted his children, and she could see the incredible tension in his face right now as he waited for her answer.

Gray wasn't just a proud, possessive male reclaiming his rights. He was a man who loved his children very deeply. Chelsea's parents had told her that over the past three years he'd made the arduous journey from Australia to America several times a year, just to see them.

Holly knew that her possibly selfish opinions about the benefits of staying in America had no place in this conversation.

She drew a deep breath. 'Anna and Josh want to be with you, Gray. You're their father.' After a beat, she added gently, 'They've missed you very much.'

His face softened a fraction. 'But it's still going to be hard for them to leave here and to make the change, isn't it?'

She couldn't deny this. 'You should probably be prepared for one or two tricky moments.'

'I was hoping that if I stayed in New York for a few days, and gave them a chance to get used to me again—'

'I'm sure that will help. And, while you're here, we can both talk to them about what to expect on the journey and when they arrive in Australia.'

Gray nodded, and let his thoughtful gaze fix on the row of windows on the opposite wall, as if he was seeing far into the distance. Then he sent Holly a slow smile.

Despite the fact that Holly was thinking about Gray's children and not his looks, something very odd happened to her insides. She dropped her gaze from the sudden flare in his light blue eyes and found safety in the tan leather duffel bag, dumped on the floor by the sofa.

It was the sort of bag that would look at home on a dusty homestead veranda, or in the back of a battered pickup. Here, in this city apartment, however, the scuffed leather holdall looked out of place, almost like a symbol of everything that had been wrong about Gray's marriage to her cousin.

Chelsea had rarely talked about the problems that had sent her scurrying home from Jabiru Creek to New York. It was clear to everyone that her decision had been painful—that she hadn't stopped loving Gray, but that she'd loved her ballet and choreography more. There'd been no jobs for a choreographer of Chelsea's calibre in Outback Australia and, in the end, she'd found it too difficult to relinquish her city life and her career.

She'd told Holly once, 'It was a fatal attraction. Gray and I were wrong for each other and in almost every way. I think we both sensed from the start that our marriage was doomed, but our feelings were so intense we still had to give it a try.'

Now, sitting mere metres from Gray Kidman's intensely masculine presence, Holly was all too aware of the force that had urged Chelsea to take that risk. He was still disturbingly attractive. Looking at him, the word *manly* seemed to take on new meaning.

Abruptly, she jumped to her feet. 'If you've finished your coffee, I'll show you to your room and you can stow your things away.'

She charged across the room, feeling a need to put a sudden distance between them.

'Holly, before you go—'

Slowly…she turned.

Gray offered a dangerously shy smile. 'I know I'm probably old-fashioned and you're a contemporary New Yorker, but I just wanted to make sure you're completely okay with having me stay here in your apartment.'

'Of course. It's perfectly fine.' Holly tried to sound off-hand. 'It makes sense.'

'And your boyfriend? Is he cool with it, too?'

A horrible knife-in-the-heart pain pierced Holly, the pain she always felt whenever Brandon was mentioned. After two months, the shock was still very raw—especially the painful discovery that Brandon had been seeing Maria Swain for six whole months before he'd found the courage to tell her.

Somehow she forced a breezy smile. 'That's not a problem. I'm between boyfriends right now.'

Not wanting to see Gray's reaction, she hurried on to the
spare room. 'It's important for you to stay here, Gray.' She
tossed the words over her shoulder. 'You need to maximise
your time with the children before you set off.'

'Thanks. I appreciate that.'

At the doorway, she stepped aside to let him into the
room. 'It's nothing special, but I guess it's adequate.'

'It's terrific.' Gray dropped his bag onto the rug at the
foot of the single bed. Holly was about to leave when he
said, 'What about you, Holly?'

'Me? Oh…my room's…um…just down the hall.'

Gray looked a tad embarrassed and scratched at the side
of his jaw. 'I wasn't asking where you sleep. I meant—
what are your plans now—once the children are off your
hands.'

'My plans? Oh…' Holly gulped. Talking to this attractive man about bedrooms must have scrambled her powers
of thinking. 'I've just finished my final exams, so I've
started sending out job applications. Who knows where
I'll end up?'

With luck, anywhere except Vermont.

Taking three quick steps backwards, she added, 'Right
now, I need to fix lunch.'

'Anything I can help with?'

'No, thanks. It's only chicken salad. You go and see the
children. Join in their game.'

Gray suggested a trip to Central Park after lunch. He always
felt more at ease entertaining his children in wide open
spaces with grass and trees and blue sky overhead, instead
of pavement and department stores and hurrying crowds.

This time, Holly came with them.

Initially Gray hadn't invited her. He'd assumed she'd be keen to grab a few hours of freedom to paint her toenails, or go shopping, or whatever city girls liked to do when they had time to themselves.

Just as the children and he were about to leave the apartment, however, Holly had handed him a pamphlet.

'This shows you everything that's going on in Central Park,' she'd said.

Gray had dismissed this with a quick, 'We'll be fine.'

Even though he was only familiar with a tiny section of Central Park, he could find the zoo, and the carousel. Anna and Josh had never complained. 'We'll play it by ear, won't we, kids?'

Holly looked surprised and she tapped a brightly coloured centre page. 'But this pamphlet lists all the children's activities. And there's a puppet theatre.'

'Puppets!' Anna and Josh both squealed in chorus. 'We want to see the puppets. Please, Daddy, please!'

Holly was still pointing to the printed page and Gray felt the first squeeze of panic. The words on the pamphlet danced and jumbled before his eyes and his chest tightened as frustration and inadequacy—two foes he'd been fighting all his life—surfaced.

'Why don't you come along with us?' he asked her then. 'And bring your pamphlet.'

Her cheeks turned pink—a very pretty pink, a perfect foil for her dark eyes and her shiny dark hair. The blush surprised Gray. Perhaps she was shyer than he'd realised.

'Yes, Holly, come with us,' Anna was pleading and grabbing her hand. 'Please, come. Please!'

Holly shook her head. 'But this is your special time to be with your daddy.'

However, she didn't need much convincing.

'Would you like me to try for last minute tickets for the

puppets?' she said next and already she was pulling her cellphone from her pocket.

They were in luck. There were four tickets available for the last performance that afternoon and when they set off for Central Park Gray noticed that Holly's shyness was quickly evaporating.

It was soon clear that she genuinely *liked* to spend time outdoors with his children. She laughed a lot and her eyes shone, and she looked somehow just right in slim blue jeans and a simple grey T-shirt, with her dark hair tied back in a ponytail and her face free of make-up.

He thought, uneasily, that his children were really going to miss Holly when it was time to leave. He couldn't help noticing how totally relaxed they were with her. Affectionate, too. Josh was perfectly happy to hold her hand when they crossed the busy streets, and Anna, all excited after a superfast slippery slide, exchanged ecstatic high fives with Holly. The gesture was so automatic and natural Gray knew they'd done this many times.

And Holly's pamphlet proved to be a great asset. It showed where the really cool playgrounds were, like the Ancient Playground based on the Egyptian Temple of Dendor, with model pyramids for climbing. And after the children had climbed and run and explored the zoo and thrown Frisbees and eaten ice creams, they all headed off to the puppet theatre in an old Swedish cottage.

The show turned out to be lively and hilarious, full of drama and excitement and silly pranks that were impossible not to enjoy.

All the children in the audience were encouraged to call out advice and warnings, so they practically lifted the roof off the ancient cottage. So very different from the serious, respectful hush of the audiences at the ballets Chelsea had dragged him to.

At one point, Gray glanced over Anna and Josh's heads and caught Holly watching him. Her dark eyes sparkled with amusement and he realised he'd been laughing out loud.

Strewth. When was the last time that had happened?

They emerged from the theatre in the late afternoon, and together they strolled through the park in the softening light of the late spring evening. The children skipped ahead, wide smiles on their faces as they imitated the Big Bad Wolf, playing hide-and-seek behind tree trunks.

His kids were okay. They were happy. And Gray discovered that he was completely and totally relaxed. He hadn't realised how tense he'd been, but now, for the first time since he'd received the shocking news about Chelsea, he was conscious of having truly unwound.

'You shouldn't have to cook again tonight,' he told Holly. 'Why don't we eat out? My shout.'

She laughed. 'I was going to suggest grabbing a meal on the way home. We have a tradition of eating out at our favourite diner on Saturday nights.'

A tradition? Gray wondered uneasily if Anna and Josh would miss these traditions. Would they be willing to help him create new traditions? He couldn't take them to a diner near his Outback home. The nearest café was a hundred kilometres from Jabiru Creek. Could a campfire on a riverbank be a reasonable substitute?

As they pushed through the swing doors of the diner on 81st Street they were greeted by laughter and happy chatter and the appetizing smells of frying bacon and coffee. The waiters recognised Holly and the children and welcomed them warmly.

Gray was introduced.

'My dad from Australia,' Josh said proudly.

They slipped into a booth with Gray and Anna on one side, Holly and Josh on the other. The waiter handed out menus.

Gray barely looked at his. 'I'll have a hamburger.'

Holly shot him a surprised glance. 'What kind of hamburger? There are at least six varieties.'

He shrugged, cracked a careless smile. 'I've worked up an appetite. Whatever's the biggest.'

'That would be the Mighty Mo,' the waiter told him with a grin.

'Thanks. Sounds perfect.' Gray turned to his daughter. 'What about you, princess? What would you like?'

He watched Anna study the menu, following down the lists with her finger.

'A grilled American cheese sandwich,' she decided.

'And I wanna hot dog,' said Josh.

'I'd like a hot dog, please, Daddy,' Holly reminded him.

'I'd like a hot dog, please, Dad.' His son sent him a cheeky grin.

'You're both excellent readers,' Gray said.

His children smiled politely, as if they were thinking— *Of course. It's only a simple old menu.*

He asked quickly, 'What are you having, Holly? Let me guess. A Greek salad?' This had always been Chelsea's choice and, judging by Holly's slim build, Gray assumed she was equally diet-conscious.

'Actually,' she replied with a raised-eyebrow smile, 'I rather fancy nachos with cheese, guacamole *and* sour cream.'

It was hours later, close to midnight, when Holly woke to the sound of high-pitched screaming. Her heart pounded as she leapt out of bed. Anna was having another nightmare.

She hurried through the apartment, not bothering to turn on a light. She was so familiar with the route from her bedroom to the children's room that she could easily dodge furniture and find her way in the dark.

But tonight, halfway down the hall, she ran into a solid object. Six feet three inches of near-naked male. Gray's warm bare chest and arms. His shoulders, bulky and smooth. His sculpted, cow-wrangling muscles. And he was only wearing boxer shorts.

'Gray.' She was suddenly breathless and flushed and—

'What's the matter with Anna?' he demanded, stepping past her.

Holly came rapidly to her senses. 'She's having a nightmare.'

As they hurried into the children's room, she gave herself a mental slap. Okay, so having a close encounter with this man's partly naked body was likely to send almost any female into a tizzy, but what had happened to her priorities? What about poor Anna?

In the children's bedroom she switched on a lamp and the room was illuminated by a soft pink glow. Anna was huddled in a tight ball in the middle of her bed, sobbing, 'Mommy! Mommy!'

Gray looked appalled and helpless, but Holly was sadly used to this scene. Kneeling on the bed, she drew the little girl into her arms. 'There, there. It's okay.' She stroked Anna's silky hair. 'It's okay, honey. You can wake up. You're all right.'

She felt the mattress dip beneath an extra weight. Gray was sitting on the other side of the bed, his eyes fierce and filled with concern. Lifting a shaking hand, he touched his daughter's tear-stained cheek.

'Anna,' he whispered. 'Anna, baby.'

'Daddy!' The little girl lifted her head from Holly's shoulder, then turned and hurled herself into her father's arms. Within minutes her shuddering sobs calmed and she buried her face into his chest.

Holly couldn't blame her. What little girl wouldn't want to be held safe in those big, strong, manly arms?

Just the same, she couldn't help feeling rejected. After weeks of comforting Anna during these middle of the night crises, Holly had suddenly become redundant.

She looked across to Josh's bed. In the early weeks he'd been the first to jump up, trying to calm his sister. Lately, he'd been more inclined to lie quietly, wide awake, knowing that Holly would come, that Holly knew what to do and that the storm would eventually pass.

'Hey there, champ,' Holly whispered.

'Hey,' the boy returned softly and then he yawned.

'You go back to sleep.' She leaned over to drop a kiss on his warm, still baby-soft cheek. He really was the greatest little guy. She adored him.

Adored them both.

When she turned back to see how Anna was now, she found Gray watching her, and it was then, in the warmth of his gaze, that she remembered that he wasn't the only adult in this room who was half undressed. She was in her thin cotton nightie—little more than a long, baggy T-shirt with a trail of dog's paw-prints stamped across her chest.

She tried to shrug off the intimacy of this situation, of being here with Gray, both in their pyjamas, tending to his children in the middle of the night. But the intimacy seemed even greater now after their afternoon in the park and their shared meal. Almost as if the four of them were a little family.

Good grief, what am I thinking?

How could she betray Chelsea with such thoughts? Very

soon she would be waving goodbye to this father and his kids. In the fall, she would embark on an exciting new career.

Enough already.

Determined to be sensible, Holly said softly, 'I think Anna will be okay now.'

In the early weeks, she'd taken the little girl back to sleep in her bed, but lately she'd been weaning Anna out of that habit.

'Perhaps she'd like a drink of water.' Holly handed Gray a glass from the nightstand and watched as Anna took a few sips. 'We can leave the lamp on for five minutes,' she said.

'Okay, princess?' Gray gently eased his daughter back into bed.

Holly pulled up the covers and tucked her in. 'Night, night.'

The little girl looked peaceful again, curled on her side, eyes closed, golden curls gleaming softly in the lamplight as she clutched her favourite fluffy koala.

Gray gave his daughter a kiss and his son a gentle shoulder thump.

''Night, Dad.'

When Gray and Holly were safely down the hallway once more, Gray let out his breath with a whoosh.

'My God,' he said quietly. 'That scared the living daylights out of me. I'd rather hear a crocodile growling at my elbow than my own daughter screaming.'

'Anna's screams are heart-rending,' Holly agreed.

'Has this been happening all along? Ever since Chelsea—?'

Holly nodded. 'It was worse at first. She's getting better. This is the first nightmare in a while.'

'Maybe she's had too much excitement for one day.'

'Perhaps that's it.'

Gray let out a heavy sigh. 'I'm sure I'm not going to be able to get back to sleep.' He ran stiff fingers through his thick dark hair. 'It's two o'clock in the afternoon where I come from. Would I disturb you too much if I made a cuppa?'

'No, not at all. Go right ahead.'

'If I make tea, would you like a cup?'

'Tea?' She laughed. 'English tea?'

He shrugged. 'English, American…I'm not fussy.'

'I'm afraid I only have green tea or camomile.'

He pulled a face. 'How about wine, then? I bought a couple of Australian reds in the duty-free.'

No, thank you.

Holly was sure she should get straight back to her room. Right now. She should not sit around in the middle of the night in her jammies having cosy chats and glasses of vino with her charges' scarily handsome father.

'I…I'd love a glass. I'll…um…just grab a wrap.'

Okay, I'm a bird-brain, but I do have a good excuse, Holly consoled herself as she hurried away. Gray needed to talk about his children. He needed to debrief after the scare he'd had with Anna.

By the time she came back into the kitchen, safely covered by a tightly knotted kimono that ended well below her knees, Gray had, mercifully, pulled on jeans and a T-shirt and he was freeing the cork from a bottle.

CHAPTER FOUR

GRAY was extremely grateful that Holly was prepared to sit and have a drink with him at midnight.

His daughter's screams had shocked him and, even though Anna had calmed quite quickly in his arms, the experience had left him feeling shaken. Anxious.

Now, more than ever, he was aware of his lack of skills. There was so much he didn't know, didn't understand about his children. He wouldn't be able to read the experts' books on psychology and grief and yet, very soon, Anna and Josh would be completely in his care.

Suddenly, his excitement over having them back in his life was mixed with terror. All his failures came back to haunt him—all the problems stemming from his childhood that had tainted his marriage.

Hell. How could he be a good single father? How could he be a role model for his kids? He'd let his parents down, let his wife down. Would he let his children down, too?

Worries chased each other, snapping like dogs at the heels of his thoughts as he and Holly sat on the corner sofas next to plate glass windows with views of the city.

They left the lamps turned low and the curtains open so they could see the black towers of the skyscrapers dotted with squares of lemon light. From below came the non-stop honk and roar of traffic. New York, the city that never sleeps.

It was a wonder anyone could ever sleep here with that constant racket, Gray thought wryly.

Holly was now wrapped in an elegant dressing gown of jade-green silk with a pattern of graceful white cranes. She sat with her bare feet tucked to one side, slim fingers curled around her glass of wine.

'It's a Margaret River red,' he said. 'Should be good. Cheers.'

She smiled faintly as she raised her glass. 'Cheers.'

They sipped the wine and shared satisfied smiles. The wine was very good.

At first they talked about practical things, about the kinds of clothes the children would need immediately in Australia, and what could be boxed for posting. There were toys to be sorted, too—favourites to go with the children now, some to be sent to charities, others to be shipped.

'How will Anna and Josh feel about leaving their friends behind?' Gray asked.

'Their school friends?' Holly shrugged. 'I don't think that will be a problem. Little kids move on. Friends come and go.' She smiled. 'Don't look so worried, Gray. Josh is cracking his neck to get to your ranch.'

Somewhat reassured, Gray had to ask the question that really bothered him. 'About Anna's nightmares—'

'Yes?'

'Do you know why she has them? Could it be because she was with Chelsea when it...when the aneurism... happened?'

'There's a good chance.' Holly dropped her gaze to her glass. 'Chelsea collapsed when she was in the middle of making Anna a peanut butter sandwich.'

It was almost too awful to imagine. Poor Anna. Poor

Chelsea. For a moment he couldn't think past the horror of it. How helpless and terrified Anna must have felt and, quite possibly, even guilty.

He sighed heavily. 'Does Josh have nightmares, too?'

Holly's dark hair rippled as she shook her head. 'I think Josh is naturally more resilient than Anna. But he rang for the ambulance, so he knows he did everything he could. I'm sure that's helped him, even if it's only at some subconscious level.'

It made sense, and the reminder of his son's quick thinking caused a small glow of pride. But poor Anna shouldn't feel guilty. 'There must be so much I need to understand. Is there anything else you should warn me about?'

Frowning, Holly took another sip of wine before she answered. 'I actually wish Josh showed more signs of grief. He's been bottling it in and I'm sure a good cry would do him good.'

'He probably thinks crying is for girls.'

'Probably. My brothers would agree.' Holly sighed. 'He probably needs to be encouraged to talk about it.'

Gray grimaced. *Talking about feelings? Sharing emotions with others?* That was so not his scene. Weren't women supposed to be so much better at it than guys? All his life, he'd been a man of action, not words.

Watching him, Holly said, 'I guess you must be very busy running your ranch. I assume you've hired a nanny to help with the children.'

'Ah…' Gray drew a sharp breath. 'So far, I've organised a team to look after the mustering, so that frees me up quite a bit. My plan was to wait till I saw Anna and Josh—and saw how they were. I thought I'd take them home, help them to settle in first, then look around for someone suitable.'

He set his empty glass on the coffee table. 'There wouldn't be any point in hiring a nanny they didn't like.'

'No. It will need to be the right person.'

Holly looked away quickly as if she didn't want him to see her eyes, but Gray was sure he'd caught a glitter of tears and his throat tightened. He'd expected her to be anxious to be free of his kids, but was she upset at the thought of saying goodbye to them?

It was so difficult for a family to span two hemispheres. There was always someone who missed out.

She turned to him again, her eyes extra-wide. 'So will Anna and Josh be involved when you choose their new nanny?'

'They'll be consulted.' Gray thought this was only fair. 'Do you have any advice?' he added, trying to be diplomatic.

'I...I'll give it some thought.' She shifted her position, uncurling her legs.

He couldn't help watching. Her legs were long and shapely and her toenails were painted a deep sexy red. In her Oriental dressing gown, with her dark hair shining in the soft light, she made a charming picture. Like a painting.

Girl at Midnight.

He thought how perfect it would be—from his children's point of view, of course—if Holly could continue on as their nanny. She understood them so well, far better than he did, and they clearly loved her. Added to that, she had teaching skills and, with her help, the transition to Australia would be almost painless.

It would never happen, of course. Holly had already told him she was about to start a new career in the US. Why would she give that up and go all the way to the Australian Outback?

She was a city girl. She was his ex-wife's cousin, for crying out loud. She was educated and cultured, just as

Chelsea had been. If she hated his place the way Chelsea had, her attitude could rub off on his kids.

Gray realised that Holly was already on her feet.

'Thanks for the wine,' she said.

'Would you like another glass?'

She shook her head. 'I need to hit the sack. Tomorrow is another day and all that.'

Her voice was tight, so tight it almost cracked. Without another word, she set the wine glass on the kitchen bench and hurried away.

She was upset. Had she been able to tell what he was thinking?

In bed, Gray lay wide awake, his thoughts running amok, trailing through the events of the day, and inevitably through the dizzying highs and lows of his romance with Chelsea. He'd met his children's mother while she was travelling in North Queensland with a touring American dance troupe, but he'd made so many mistakes...so many wrong turns...

He'd never seen a girl so delicate and fair, so perfectly beautiful in every way. He'd never looked into a woman's eyes and fallen from a great height.

It had been a classic case of love at first sight, with all the usual symptoms—the thunderbolt to the heart, the obsession.

With the recklessness of youth, Gray had followed Chelsea back to America. In New York he'd courted her with the single-minded passion of a young man desperately in love. A hasty engagement, a wedding in Central Park and a blissful honeymoon in Paris...

Then back to Jabiru Creek Station. To the Outback.

Within the first month, Chelsea had realised her mistake. She'd loved Gray—about that there had never been any doubt—but in the Australian Outback his precious bride had wilted like a flower without water.

His throat ached now as he remembered the tears streaming down her face as she'd confronted him.

We've made a mistake, Gray, haven't we? Don't you think we should separate now, before this gets too complicated? You're a good man. I should have been more honest. I didn't want to hurt you.

Of course, he should have given in then. It was so easy now to look back and to see how foolish and blinded he'd been—how he'd kissed her tears and begged her shamelessly.

You must stay, Chelsea. Please, please give it a go.

It was only a few weeks later that she'd realised she was pregnant so, of course, she'd stayed...

'You wake him up.'

'No, you.'

Childish giggling penetrated Gray's sleep. *Damn.* Was it morning already?

It had taken him hours to fall asleep and he felt absolutely stuffed, unable to move, like an elephant paralysed by a stun gun. Perhaps, if he lay very still, his children would creep away again and leave him to sleep.

Not a chance. Already small hands were poking and shaking him.

'Dad! Dad!'

He groaned in a low protest.

'Daddy!' That was Anna's voice, now suddenly panic-stricken.

His eyes snapped open, then he cringed from the bright daylight flooding the room. 'Good morning,' he groaned. 'What time is it?'

'It's really late,' Josh told him. 'We had breakfast ages and ages ago.'

Gray struggled onto one elbow, yawned and rubbed a hand over sleep-bleary eyes.

'Are you all right, Daddy?' Anna still sounded worried.

'Yeah, chicken. I'm fine.' He yawned again. 'Just sleepy. My body thinks it's still in Australia.'

He swung his legs over the side of the bed and sat for a minute, elbows propped on his knees, holding his dazed head in his hands. Jet lag was taking its toll.

'Holly said to tell you she's made a fresh pot of coffee,' Josh announced.

Bless Holly. Coffee was exactly what he needed. As soon as he'd had a shower.

Gray ruffled his kids' hair. 'So what have you two got planned for today?'

'Packing!' they chorused.

'You're kidding?' How could they look so excited? 'Don't tell me packing's fun?'

'Sure, Dad. It's great fun. Holly's playing a new game with us. We're putting all our toys in a magic rocket box, and it's going to take off for Australia all by itself.'

'Wow. How about that?'

Gray had to hand it to Holly. She sure had a way with his kids. Damn pity she wasn't coming home with them.

As the hot water in the shower streamed over him, he reminded himself why he mustn't put any pressure on Holly to help him out. She'd already gone above and beyond for his children, and now she had a life of her own to lead. Holly was a good sport and she would never let on that she was cracking her neck to be free of her commitments here. But he knew she must be keen to get on with her new career and to start dating again, find a new boyfriend.

He wouldn't appeal to her good nature...couldn't exploit her genuine affection for his kids by trying to talk her into coming with them. That would be nothing short of emotional blackmail.

Just the same, Gray wished he felt more confident in his ability to raise his kids.

Their education was his major worry.

For all kinds of reasons Gray's own parents had totally stuffed up his schooling. Just thinking about his lack of education triggered unwelcome memories of his parents' harsh and heated bickering. He found himself remembering his mother's fits of crying and his father's sulky, blustering anger and his innards twisted.

Truth to tell, his formal schooling had finished almost as soon as it started, around the same time as his parents' divorce. However, it was only much later in his adult years that Gray had fully understood the handicap he carried. By then he'd developed a tough veneer and he'd managed to bluff his way through most challenges, never realising that his failings would come back to bite him, that he'd let his wife down...

And now he was in danger of letting his kids down...

No. There was no way he would allow Anna and Josh to grow up with the limitations he'd endured. But if he wanted to give them the very best chance, he needed help. He needed someone exactly like Holly.

If only she was free...

We've done well, Holly thought at the end of a full day of packing and, thanks to Gray's involvement, it had been relatively painless. Gray's sense of humour—a side of him she'd never really seen before—had saved a few awkward moments when decisions over toys might have ended in tears.

And then he'd surprised her further by cooking dinner.

'Because you've been working so hard,' he'd said with an endearingly shy smile that sent her stomach fluttering. 'And only if you like spaghetti bolognese. I'm afraid there's a limit to my kitchen skills.'

Spaghetti bolognese was absolutely fine, Holly assured him. Unfortunately, anything seemed fine when he sent her those smiles.

Except she didn't want to be susceptible to his smiles, did she? She was simply grateful for the chai latte he'd brought her from the drugstore two and a half blocks away, as well as the chance to soak in the tub and change her clothes before dinner, and then enjoy a meal she hadn't had to cook.

Over dinner, Anna and Josh talked about Australia. They were very excited to hear that Gray had an airstrip on his property and that his mail and supplies were delivered by aeroplane.

'We'll fly to Normanton,' Gray explained, 'and then we'll drive home to Jabiru from there.'

We'll drive home to Jabiru...

Holly pictured Gray and his children in a big SUV, skimming over wide red plains towards a distant homestead, and she was swamped by a wave of loneliness.

What was wrong with her? She'd known all along that this would happen. But she still couldn't help feeling miserable. Everyone who was important in her life was being taken from her—Chelsea, Brandon, and now Anna and Josh.

I'll start again and build a new life around my new job.

Right now, it was hard to feel happy about that.

Suddenly she realised Josh was asking his dad about their new school.

To Holly's surprise, Gray's ears reddened. He looked pained and cleared his throat. 'The school in the Outback is a bit different from what you're used to.'

'How different?'

'It's called School of the Air.'

'School of the Air?' This time it was Holly who butted in. She couldn't help it. Her interest was thoroughly piqued. 'How does that work?'

Gray smiled crookedly. 'It's like a normal classroom, but the classes are held over the radio. There are children living in homesteads scattered all over the Outback and each homestead has a special transceiver. They send messages back and forth. The teacher can talk to all of the pupils and they can talk to each other.' He shrugged. 'It seems to work really well.'

'School over the radio? Wow. That sounds totally awesome.' Josh couldn't have looked more excited if he'd been told there were pet baby dinosaurs at his new school.

'It sounds amazing,' Holly agreed, thoroughly intrigued. To her surprise, she felt quite jealous of the nanny who would mentor Anna and Josh as they came to grips with this unorthodox schoolroom.

She shot the children sparkling grins. 'Aren't you two lucky?'

Josh, twirling spaghetti onto his fork, nodded enthusiastically.

Anna, however, looked uncertain. She turned to Holly. 'Will you still be our nanny?'

Holly held her breath, not trusting herself to answer this question without giving her feelings away.

To her relief, Gray answered for her. 'Holly can't come

to Australia, Anna. You know that. But we're going to find a nice Australian nanny.'

Anna drooped. 'I want Holly. And I like my school here. Why do you have to live in Australia? Why can't you live in New York?'

Holly saw the sudden bleakness in Gray's eyes, the wavering of his smile. Even though he'd sounded confident about finding a *nice Australian nanny,* he was obviously worried by Anna's reaction.

She'd been determined to keep out of this conversation, but her heart was melting at the sight of Gray's discomfort and she felt compelled to jump to his aid.

'How could your dad live in this apartment?' she asked with a deliberate smile. 'What would he do with all his cattle?'

Anna shrugged. 'Put them in storage?'

'As if.' Josh groaned and rolled his eyes.

An awkward hush fell. Gray continued to look worried and Anna looked as if she might cry. Her lower lip trembled.

Watching her, Josh began to look anxious, too. 'It's going to be great living with Dad,' he urged his sister softly.

'Not if Holly can't come with us.'

Holly saw Gray's shoulders stiffen at the same moment she felt her face flame.

Then Anna burst into tears.

'Hey,' Holly said, quickly drawing the little girl onto her lap, and not daring to catch Gray's eyes again. 'How can you cry in the middle of this lovely dinner your dad has cooked?'

Anna's response was to cling to Holly tightly, sobbing louder than ever. 'Why can't you come with us?'

It was a truly difficult moment. Holly knew Gray was anxious about his ability to care for his fragile daughter and now her tearful reaction would only deepen his apprehension.

But, despite this, Holly couldn't help feeling electrified, too, as if she'd touched a live wire. Anna had innocently brought into the open the very question that had rattled around in her head all day.

The thing was—school in the US didn't start again till the autumn, which meant she could spend June and July in Australia helping the children to settle in to their new home and school, and she'd still be back in time to start her new teaching job.

And now that she'd heard about this School of the Air, the idea was especially intriguing.

Of course, it wouldn't be plain sailing. After the past hectic months she would have liked a proper vacation and, if she went to Australia, she'd still be 'working'. She'd have very little chance to catch her breath before she had to start in the new school.

Then again, she didn't have any particular plans for the next few weeks—and she certainly didn't fancy going home to Vermont, where she'd spend her time either avoiding Brandon or being showered with sympathy from family and friends. And she *was* intrigued by the set-up in the Outback—and, of course, she would love to see Anna and Josh happily settled.

The only negative factor was the silly frissons that danced over her skin whenever Gray Kidman came too near—but Holly was sure she'd soon conquer that foolish tendency.

For heaven's sake, there wasn't any danger she'd actually fall for poor Chelsea's ex when the pain of being dumped by Brandon hadn't even healed. She planned to be mega-cautious around all men in future—especially the attractive ones.

* * *

'Why don't you tuck the children into bed and read them a couple of stories?' Holly suggested to Gray after dinner.

To her surprise, he looked unhappy, as if she'd asked him to help with some horrible chore like cleaning the toilets with a toothbrush.

'But won't they expect you to do it?' he asked.

His obvious nervousness puzzled Holly. Perhaps Anna's tears at dinner had upset him more than she'd realised. She tried to reassure him. 'Anna and Josh will love it if you read to them tonight.'

When Gray still looked worried, she added, 'They need to get used to small changes, and this would be a good first step.'

He swallowed uncomfortably. 'I guess.'

'Their favourite books are stacked on the nightstand.'

'Okay.'

As he left the kitchen, heading for the children's room, Holly saw a deep red tide that was *not* sunburn staining the back of his neck. The sight of it caused an ache right in the centre of her chest. Was he nervous about being alone with his children? Was he afraid Anna would cry again? Should she have offered to be there, too?

She almost called out to him, but there was something about the resolute straightness of his shoulders and the purposeful length of his stride that stopped her. He was like a soldier marching off to war. No, she was being fanciful.

And in the end everything was fine.

While Holly cleared the table and stacked the dishwasher, she could hear the deep masculine rumble of Gray's voice and the bell-like tinkle of the children's laughter. They were clearly having a great time.

With the kitchen tidy, she went into the living room and tried to relax, curled on the sofa with her current paperback novel. As soon as Gray was finished with the bedtime stories, she would talk to him about Australia. She only wished the thought of their conversation didn't make her feel so inordinately excited.

It was quite a while before Gray returned, however, and he was smiling, his blue eyes reflecting relief and a new contentment.

'That seemed to go well,' Holly said warmly.

'Yeah.' He stood in the centre of the room, hands resting lightly on his hips, and he grinned. 'Seems like I passed my first test as a single dad.'

'That's great. I suppose Josh pressured you into reading the pirate story.'

'No, actually. I told them a completely different story tonight.'

'Oh, right.' She couldn't help asking. 'Which one?'

Gray shrugged. 'I made one up. About Hector Owl and Timothy Mouse.' He shot her a shrewdly narrowed glance. 'Your experts wouldn't object, would they?'

'N-no, of course not. I'm just surprised. Amazed, actually. I've loved stories all my life but, even if you paid me thousands, I couldn't make one up on the spot. Anna and Josh seemed to love yours.'

Still standing in the middle of the living room carpet, Gray shrugged again and scratched at the shadow of stubble on his jaw, then he quickly changed the subject. 'Fancy another glass of that wine we opened last night?'

'Why not?' Wine might help to steady her nerves.

While he collected the bottle and glasses, Holly set her book aside and stood quickly, taking a surreptitious peek at her reflection in the long mirror on the opposite wall. It was silly. Really, she knew the neatness of her hair, the fit of her jeans or the flounces on her cream silk blouse were of no interest to Gray. But the conversation she was about to launch was almost a job interview. Checking her appearance was an automatic reflex.

'You look great,' Gray said, coming back into the room more quickly than she expected.

Flustered, she fought off a blush and sat quickly, wishing she could think of a witty retort.

'No, honestly, that new hairstyle suits you,' he said, handing her a glass of the rich Australian red.

A trip to the hairdresser had been part of Holly's post-Brandon recovery plan, but she was amazed that Gray had noticed.

'Thanks.' She raised her glass. 'Here's to settling the twins happily in Australia. May it all go super-smoothly.'

'Amen to that.' Gray settled into an armchair and stretched his long legs in front of him, crossing them at the ankles.

Holly tried not to stare, but Gray had a way of catching her eye. His jeans were soft and worn and faded, hugging his strong thighs. His elastic-sided boots were tan and clean and made of finely cut leather. Lamplight caught the dark sheen of his hair and accented the ruggedly masculine planes and angles of his face and the shadow on his jaw.

There was no denying the man was bone-deep sexy. At Chelsea's wedding, even Holly's grandmother had been all girlish and coy in Gray's presence.

Perhaps she shouldn't say anything about Australia after all. She didn't want to spend the next couple of months stealing sneak peeks at Chelsea's ex just because she was currently without a boyfriend. She was supposed to be getting on with her exciting new single life, making plans for her brilliant career.

She drank some wine, buying time to compose herself, but her brain refused to let go of one particular thought and suddenly the words just tumbled out. 'I've been thinking that you might need help with the children when you first arrive in Australia.'

Gray nodded calmly. 'I've been thinking the same thing. I wondered if I should phone ahead to an employment agency.'

'An agency in Australia?'

'Yes.'

Holly felt a surge of emotion, almost panic. 'I'm at a loose end.'

Oh, cringe. How annoying that she could say something in her head all day and it sounded fine, but now, as soon as she said it out loud, it sounded utterly dumb.

It didn't help that Gray's head snapped back as if he'd been punched in the jaw. He was staring at her as if she'd announced she was planning to fly into outer space. On a broomstick.

'How do you mean—a loose end?' he asked quietly.

'I'm free—for a month or so.'

'I thought you were starting work in a school.'

Holly's mouth was suddenly parched. She took a sip from her glass and to her dismay her hand was shaking. 'The schools here are about to close for the summer.' She wished her voice wasn't shaking as well. She cleared her throat. 'I wouldn't be expected to start in a new job until August, or possibly September.'

His eyes widened. 'So you're free through the rest of June and July?'

'As long as I'm still in phone or Internet contact. For interviews.' Seeing the surprise in Gray's eyes, Holly's nervousness accelerated. 'It's just a thought. A possible option.'

'But it's a fantastic option.' His eyes were gleaming, and his face broke into a fully fledged smile. 'You'd be perfect.'

For God's sake, stay cool.

'Do you have a passport?' Gray asked, clearly thinking more calmly than she was.

Holly nodded. She'd studied Italian at school and her parents had scraped and saved to send her on a fabulous school excursion to Tuscany. Her passport was still valid.

Gray's smile was replaced by a quick frown. 'Are you sure you wouldn't mind giving up so much time?'

'I'd be happy to come. I'm really interested in this School of the Air. I'd love to see how it works and, of course, I'd really like to help Anna and Josh to settle in.'

Gray was frowning again and he launched to his feet, pacing the room as if something troubled him. 'I promise you'd have nothing to worry about—' He swallowed and looked awkward. 'I mean—accompanying me and the kids—no one out there will jump to conclusions about us. I...I mean no one will assume we're a couple.'

Looking distinctly embarrassed, he gave a forced laugh, as if he was trying to make a joke but knew it wasn't funny.

To Holly's dismay, she felt her face flame. 'Well, that's good,' she hurried to assure him. 'And you certainly don't need to worry from my end. Romance is totally off my agenda. I've just broken up a long-term relationship, and it was harrowing to say the least, so it'll be a very long time before I start looking for any kind of—' She couldn't quite finish the sentence.

Gray nodded thoughtfully, his eyes sending a message of sympathy, and Holly felt a clear wave of relief to know that they had the ground rules sorted.

Just the same, she couldn't help also feeling the teensiest sting over Gray's mega-eagerness to make it clear that he wasn't romantically interested in her.

How crazy was that? She dropped her gaze to her wine

and reminded herself exactly why she'd made this offer. Gray needed help, Anna and Josh needed a nanny, and she needed to feel she'd done everything she could for Chelsea's children.

She was the perfect person to help Anna and Josh to adjust to their new life in Australia.

'So that's definite, then?' Gray was serious again. Businesslike. 'You'll come?'

Suddenly it felt inevitable. Predestined. As if this question was always going to be asked. And the answer was always going to be...

'Yes.'

CHAPTER FIVE

GRAY was surprised by how over-the-top pleased and light-hearted he felt now that he knew Holly would be accompanying them on the return journey.

Now, the challenge of becoming a single father no longer loomed as forbidding as Mount Everest and, over the following days as they finalised the packing, even Anna came to look on the move as a huge adventure.

By the time the foursome reached JFK Airport, they were all keyed up and looking forward to the flight.

It was while they were waiting to get through Security, with the line shuffling ever closer to the X-ray machines, that Holly received a call on her cellphone.

Gray assumed it was yet another of her many friends ringing to wish her well and he watched with a ready smile as she answered the phone. He saw the sudden tension in her eyes.

She turned away, her dark hair swinging with the movement. She pressed her fingers to one ear to block out the airport noise as she frowned and gave her caller her full attention.

Gray realised he was watching her more closely than was polite, but he couldn't help it. Holly might not have Chelsea's beauty, but she had something else—something, he suspected, more lasting than prettiness. At times like now, when her face was animated and her dark eyes were sparkling with excitement, she looked utterly enchanting.

Snatches of her conversation drifted his way.

'Yes...yes...that's wonderful...yes. Oh, wow, thank you.' And then, 'Australia...a family commitment...just away for the summer...' She was nodding and smiling, looking flushed and pleased.

The phone call ended just as it was their turn to go through Security, so it wasn't till they'd reached the other side and had collected their watches, wallets, passports and backpacks that Holly turned to Gray with a wide and happy smile.

'So it was good news after all?' he asked.

'Yes. At first I thought it might have been Brand—might have been someone ringing to say goodbye. But it's even better than that. It looks like I've landed a job.'

To Gray's surprise, he felt a snaking of alarm. How would this affect their plans? Was Holly still free to help? 'When do you start?'

'Not till August.' Holly's smile widened into a beaming grin, then she gave a little skip and punched the air. 'I can't believe it. This is my dream job! My first choice. The school I've always wanted to teach at.'

Gray nodded, willing himself to be pleased for Holly. Judging by her excitement, this was very important. She must have been the pick of the applicants. Good for her!

It hit him then that he knew very little about her. It seemed she was very smart—an ace teacher—and his kids were lucky to have her even for a short time.

He was pleased for her. In fact, he was pleased for all of them. Everything was working out perfectly. By August his children would be settled into their new home and school and, with Holly's help and approval, he'd have hired a new nanny. Then Holly would head for home to start this new flash job.

It made absolutely no sense that he couldn't dredge up more enthusiasm. It was sheer selfishness not to be happy for Holly.

'Fantastic,' he said and he held out his hand. 'Congratulations.'

At last, he cracked a smile.

Landing in Sydney was a total surprise for Holly.

Throughout the journey, she'd been mentally preparing herself for the Australian Outback. It was, she knew, a challenging place of wide red plains, isolation, dust and heat.

She hadn't given much thought to Sydney, hadn't expected to fly in over gorgeous golden beaches to a big and modern city heart crowded with skyscrapers. She also hadn't expected to find Gray's mother waiting to greet them at Sydney Airport.

Holly had vague memories of Sasha Carlisle from the wedding. She was tall and silver-haired, strikingly attractive and well dressed. Today she was wearing a white linen trouser suit, with sparkling jewellery at her wrist and a long black and white silk scarf draped with unfussy elegance. There was no doubt about it; she'd nailed casual chic for the older woman.

Beside her, Holly, in jeans and a crumpled T-shirt, with her hair hanging limp after more than twenty hours in a pressurised cabin, felt decidedly drab. But she soon forgot about that as she watched the greeting between mother and son.

No warm hugs. Just a cool—

'Hello, dear.'

'Hello, Mother.'

And an expertly made-up cheek held at an angle for Gray to kiss.

The tension was so thick Holly would have needed a very sharp knife to cut through it. It evaporated quickly, however, when Gray's mother turned her attention to her grandchildren.

'Sweethearts,' she cried, opening her arms to Anna and Josh. 'You remember your Australian granny, don't you?'

Fortunately, the children obliged her with warm smiles, and they submitted to hugs and kisses without complaint.

'Your granny's missed you so much.'

Brightly wrapped packages were produced from a voluminous designer handbag, and Holly was pleased to see that Anna and Josh looked quite thrilled and remembered to say thank you.

Gray placed a hand on Holly's shoulder, almost making her jump out of her skin. 'You might not remember my mother, Sasha Carlisle.'

With her shoulder still tingling from the warmth of his touch, Holly held out her hand. 'I do remember you, Mrs Carlisle. How do you do?'

Gray's mother shook hands super-carefully, as if she were afraid Holly might be grubby.

'Holly was one of Chelsea's bridesmaids,' Gray reminded her.

'Ah, yes, and now she's the nanny.'

'Holly's going to help us with School of the Air,' Josh explained importantly.

'Is she now?' Sasha's eyebrows lifted high and she shot a chilling but meaningful glance to Gray. 'Is she properly trained?'

Bristling at being discussed as if she wasn't even there,

Holly decided to speak up for herself. 'I'm a fully qualified English teacher.'

The older woman smiled faintly. 'Thank heavens for small mercies.'

What was going on here?

The chilling tension was broken by Anna, who urgently wanted to find a bathroom. Grateful to escape, Holly accompanied her and, by the time they returned, Sasha had left.

'My mother had a function she needed to attend,' Gray said smoothly. The expression in his eyes lightened and he smiled at Holly. 'Come on, let's find a taxi.'

Their evening in Sydney was fun. The four of them dined out at a fabulous Thai restaurant and then they walked back to their hotel, enjoying the mild winter night and the brightly lit streets. The children were drooping by this stage, however, and Gray had to carry Anna for the last block. She and Josh were so tired they fell straight into bed and were asleep before anyone could think of finding a story to read.

Gray stayed behind to share a nightcap with Holly in the cosy sitting room that was part of the luxurious suite he'd booked for her and the children.

They found ice and glasses and little bottles in the mini-bar and then they sat in deep comfy armchairs. Holly wasn't sure how relaxed she'd be, or what she and Gray would talk about, so she was totally thrown when he steered the conversation to her break-up with Brandon.

'What went wrong?' he asked, watching her through slightly narrowed eyes.

'Oh, the usual.' Holly had only talked about her break-up with her mom and one or two girlfriends, and it felt weird to try to explain it to a man she hardly knew. 'He was more interested in another woman.'

'So he was a fool,' Gray said sympathetically.

'Yes, he was a total idiot.' She forced a smile. 'But it was partly my fault, I guess. I moved away to New York and, in this case, absence did not make his heart grow fonder.'

Gray nodded and took a thoughtful sip of his drink. 'Don't know if it helps...but after Chelsea took off with the kids...I thought I'd never get over it, and yet, after a time, the worst feelings began to fade.'

Holly wanted to ask him what had gone wrong in his marriage, but it felt too intrusive to ask Gray when Chelsea had been so close-lipped about it.

Instead, she said, 'I guess Chelsea must have loved it here in Sydney.'

Gray's smile vanished as if someone had flicked a switch. 'I'm sure Chelsea must have told you how she felt about Sydney.'

'No.' Holly blinked. 'If she did, I don't remember. She would never say much at all about her time in Australia.'

He downed a hefty slug of Scotch and scowled into his glass, and Holly felt compelled to explain her comment. 'It's just that I was surprised to see how busy and cosmopolitan it is here. Bright lights. Masses of skyscrapers. Lots of people. So many theatres and restaurants. It's everything Chelsea loved.'

She watched Gray's mouth thin into a downward curve.

He sighed. 'Yeah, Chelsea loved Sydney all right. She used to fly down here for two or three days and stay for two or three weeks.'

'Oh.' Sensing that she'd awoken bad memories, Holly tried to make amends. 'I suppose she dropped in to chat to the dance companies here and—'

Suddenly, she wasn't sure how to finish what she'd started. She was trying to defend her cousin when she had no idea really...

'This place had *everything* Chelsea needed,' Gray said bleakly.

Holly wondered if this had been the heart of the problem with their marriage. 'Did you ever—' she began hesitantly. 'I mean, I don't suppose you...um...considered moving here? Or...or living closer...'

'No.'

There was quiet vehemence in that single syllable. Gray's face was a grim stony mask as he stared down at his almost empty glass.

'I guess it would have been difficult to move.'

She was trying to be diplomatic, but she knew she was on shaky ground. Just the same, she couldn't help thinking that if Gray had really loved Chelsea he might have been prepared to make sacrifices. Couldn't he have given up cattle farming and tried something more suited to his wife's temperament and talents?

If he'd wanted to save his marriage...

'Moving was out of the question,' he said with a marked air of finality.

Right.

It was time to drop this line of conversation. Holly wondered if stubborn inflexibility was Gray Kidman's Achilles heel.

Or was that a bit harsh? After all, her cousin had been adamant when she married him that she was happy to give up her career to live with him in his Outback.

Whatever. It's none of my business.

To change the subject, Holly said, 'I'm looking forward to tomorrow and finally getting to see your place.'

She saw Gray's shoulders relax then, and he looked

directly into her eyes and smiled slowly in a way that started her tummy fluttering. 'So am I,' he said. 'I'm always glad to get home.'

The warmth in his eyes suggested that he wasn't just voicing a cliché. He really meant it. He felt nostalgic about his home in the vast empty Outback. Holly understood this. She always felt a catch in her throat whenever she drove back to her family's farm and saw the green pastures and red barns of Vermont.

Tomorrow Anna and Josh would reach their new home. Holly hoped, for their sakes, but more especially for Gray's sake, that they liked it. Actually, it was her job to make sure that they did.

Gray couldn't sleep.

Leaving his bed, he prowled the length of his hotel room, trying to shrug off the tension that kept him awake. He'd lied to Holly tonight. He'd told her that feelings and memories faded with time but, after his mother's cool reception at the airport today, and his conversation with Holly about Chelsea, he was once again battling with the feelings of inadequacy and failure that had dogged him all his life.

As a child he'd never lived up to his mother's expectations. Hell, he hadn't even come close. He could still hear the way she'd yelled at his father.

The boy's hopeless. Unteachable. A disgrace.

Even now, the memory brought his clenched fist slamming into his palm.

Was he never going to shake off these patterns of failure? First his mother had left Jabiru, never to return, and then his wife had left, and both times he'd known he was a major cause of their problems.

If he'd been able to, he would have taken Chelsea to live in Sydney, as Holly had so innocently suggested. He would have taken her to New York or wherever she wanted to live.

But, thanks to his lack of schooling, he was unemployable in the city, and even if he'd sold his property and invested in stocks and shares to eke out a living, he would have gone mad in the claustrophobic city. After twenty-four hours, he was always chafing at the bit to get away to the bush.

He'd tried his best to love and support Chelsea at Jabiru. When the twins arrived, he'd done everything he could to hold his little family together. He'd been a hands-on father, taking his turn at bathing and changing and walking the floors with the crying infants.

But the timing had been lousy. The babies' arrival had coincided with a downturn in the cattle industry. Overseas markets had collapsed. Money had been tight and, before the babies were six months old, he'd been forced to lay off the fencing contractors and the mechanics he'd hired, and he'd taken on these jobs himself.

When these tasks were added to the usual demands of running a vast cattle property, his available time to help at the homestead had been minimal. He'd kept on his housekeeper, who'd also helped with the twins, but the toll on Chelsea had been visible.

Gray had been shocked to see her growing thin and drawn and faded, so he'd sent her to Sydney for short breaks. And, as he'd admitted to Holly, the times she'd spent away had become longer and longer.

When his wife had told him she needed to go home to New York, he'd let her go, taking the children with her, even though he hadn't been free to accompany them. By then he'd known that to try to hold her was too cruel.

When she'd rung from New York to tell him she wasn't coming back, Gray had been heartsick but not surprised.

He'd agreed to the divorce, accepting that he'd had no other option.

He'd tried his hardest and failed, and he had no idea what else he could do. He would rather admit defeat than watch his wife become trapped and embittered the way his mother had been.

But his sense of failure was overwhelming, even worse now that Chelsea had passed away. He hated to think that his love had made any part of her short life unhappy and he was determined that he wouldn't fail her children as well. He couldn't, he mustn't.

These next two months were critical. He would be guided by Holly and he wouldn't be too proud to accept her advice. Sure, there were bound to be humiliating moments when his inadequacies were exposed once more, and Holly would probably be as disdainful of his home as Chelsea had been.

But he could face another woman's scorn—as long as his kids still looked up to him—and as long as he didn't let them down.

By the following afternoon, they were finally in Far North Queensland, barrelling over flat, pale grasslands in a big four-wheel drive which threw up a continuous plume of dust. The vehicle had a luggage rack on top, and bull bars protecting the engine—from kangaroos, Gray told them—and there were water tanks on board as well. To Holly it felt like an expedition.

Wide open plains sprinkled with straggly gum trees and silvery grey Brahman cattle stretched in every direction. Flocks of white birds wheeled in the blue sky like fluttering pieces of paper.

In the back seat, the children watched the panorama excitedly, waiting for their first kangaroo sighting.

'This is my country,' Gray told Holly and his emphasis on the word *country* seemed to instil it with special meaning.

Holly had to agree there was something primitive but almost spiritual about the vast stretch of empty space. She could feel an awareness of something greater than herself and, strangely, it wasn't unlike the way she'd also felt the first time she'd walked into the huge book-lined silence of the New York City Library.

Every so often their vehicle would climb over a rocky ridge, giving a view of grasslands stretching for ever. At other times the road would dip downwards to cross a single lane wooden bridge over a stream. Some creeks only had a concrete ford disappearing beneath brown muddy water.

'There's no water here at all in the dry season,' Gray told her.

They came to a wider river, so deep that when Gray pushed the vehicle through, the water threatened to seep under the doors.

He grinned at Holly. 'This is where I did my ankle in, but the creek was flowing a lot faster then, of course.'

The tops of the banks were still covered in flattened grass and the small twisted trees were all leaning in one direction, clear evidence of how high and savage the floodwaters had been.

Holly hated to think what it must have been like to try to drive through it.

'I thought you had an airstrip at Jabiru,' she said. 'Couldn't you have flown instead of driving?'

Gray shook his head. 'The ground was too boggy for a normal plane to land—and all the choppers were needed for emergency rescues. I waited for the water to go down a little, then took my chances.'

How scary. Holly shuddered, as she tried to imagine pushing a vehicle through a raging flood.

'And that was when you broke your ankle?' she asked.

'I was testing the bottom before I drove across. Foot went down into a crevice.'

'You weren't on your own, were you?'

'Sure.'

'You mean you had to rescue yourself?'

'It was either that or—' He flicked a glance over his shoulder and dropped his voice. 'Or this pair would have been orphans.'

Holly shivered, chastened to remember how she'd rolled her eyes and complained loudly when Gray had telephoned to say he was held up in Australia by floods and a broken ankle. Now that she was here, and could see where the accident had happened, she was appalled.

No wonder Gray gave off an aura of hidden toughness and competence.

As they cleared the creek and continued over flat land again, squawks from the back seat reminded Holly of her duties. Anna and Josh were pinching each other and poking out tongues. Clear signs of boredom. Very soon they'd start, *Are we there yet?*

She rummaged in her bag and produced a CD. 'This might keep them entertained,' she said, waving it at Gray.

'Good idea. What is it?'

'Winnie-the-Pooh.'

His brow wrinkled. 'Never heard of them. Are they a new band?'

She laughed. 'Oh, that's a good one.'

He turned, sending her a puzzled grin. 'Seriously, who are they?'

Her mouth dropped open. How could he ask? 'You know Winnie-the-Pooh—the children's story. You must have read it when you were little. The bear who loves honey.'

He pulled a face and shrugged. 'Whatever. We've got about three-quarters of an hour to go, so if you think it will keep the kids happy, bung it on.'

Bemused, she slipped the CD into the player and soon the cabin was filled with the storyteller's beautifully modulated English voice. The children stopped squabbling and listened. Gray seemed to listen attentively, too, and he actually chuckled at the antics of the famous characters as if the funny bits were a brand new experience for him.

How curious.

The CD hadn't finished when they turned in at big metal gates beneath an overhead sign with *Jabiru Creek* painted in white.

'We're here!' Anna cried enthusiastically. 'This is your place, isn't it, Daddy?'

'That's right, pumpkin, but we're not at the homestead yet. It's about another fifteen minutes.'

Resigned, the children slumped back in their seats.

'I'll get the gates,' Holly announced, opening her passenger door.

Gray's eyebrows shot high. 'You don't have to.'

'It's fine,' she called over her shoulder as she jumped down from the vehicle. 'I'm a farm girl.'

She turned, saw the surprise in his blue eyes.

'When were you on a farm?'

'I grew up on a farm in Vermont.'

Through the dusty windscreen she saw his smile and a new light in his eyes—keen interest, extra warmth. She blushed and felt flustered. *Idiot.* Abruptly, she turned and paid studious attention to the gates.

By the time the gates were shut once more and she'd

climbed back in the cabin, Gray was closing his satellite phone. 'I let them know at the homestead that we're nearly home. Almost time to put the kettle on.'

Anna leaned forward as far as her seatbelt would allow. 'Will we see the puppies? Are they borned yet, Daddy?'

'Sorry, I forgot to ask.' Gray grinned back at his daughter. 'You'll soon find out.'

They drove on and the CD resumed, preventing conversation or questions about Holly's life on the farm. But Holly couldn't stop thinking about the surprised delight in Gray's eyes. Why should it matter where she'd grown up?

The bush was thicker now, and the gum trees threw shadows across the narrow wheel ruts that formed the rough track. Several times, Gray had to brake suddenly as a kangaroo appeared on the edge of the road, bounding unannounced from a shadowy clump of trees.

Each kangaroo sighting was a source of huge excitement for Holly and the children, but Holly could tell that the animals' sudden arrival on the track was dangerous. In the fading light they were hard to see. She switched off the CD so Gray could concentrate.

'That wasn't a bad story,' he said. Then he called over his shoulder, 'Hey, kids, what do you reckon? Is that Pooh bear almost as good as Hector Owl and Timothy Mouse?'

'Nah. Winnie-the-Pooh's for babies,' Josh replied, even though he'd spent the best part of an hour listening to the CD quite happily. 'Hector Owl's much better. Hector Owl's awesome. He killed the Bad Bush Rat.'

Holly smiled. How could poor Winnie compete with a murderous owl?

But it still puzzled her that Gray spoke as if he'd never heard of Winnie-the-Pooh. How could that be? Surely almost every child in the US and Australia was familiar with the honey-loving bear.

Should she be dreading what lay ahead? Would Gray's house be as stark and unappealing as that lonely homestead on the back of the playing cards he'd bought?

She was about to find out.

Ahead of them, the track rounded a corner and they emerged into open country once more. Holly saw tall corrals and stockyards, home paddocks fenced with timber instead of the barbed wire she'd seen everywhere else. Then, ahead, more buildings began to appear—machinery sheds, silos, bunk houses, barns, even an aircraft hangar—it was almost a small village.

Clearly Jabiru Creek Station was a much bigger concern than the farms she was used to.

'Which one is your house, Daddy?' Anna wanted to know.

'That place straight ahead with the silver roof.' Gray pointed to a long, low, white timber building surrounded by surprisingly green lawns.

To Holly's relief, Gray's home looked inviting. It was a simple homestead, but it was large and rimmed by verandas. Across the front of the house a deep shady veranda was fringed with hanging baskets filled with ferns, while the verandas on either side were enclosed from floor to ceiling with white timber louvres.

The lawns in front of the house were divided by a gravel path and on either side stood massive shade trees with deep glossy foliage.

'I can see a swing,' Anna shouted, pointing to a rubber tyre hanging by thick ropes from the branch of one of the trees.

'It's waiting for you,' Holly told her, and already she was picturing Anna and Josh playing on this smooth sweep of lawn, swinging in the tyre, riding bikes, throwing balls, chasing puppies...

The front door opened and a woman came out with a beaming smile, wiping her hands on an apron. She was aged somewhere beyond sixty and was dressed in a floral cotton dress, with wisps of grey hair escaping from a haphazard knot on top of her head.

'My housekeeper, Janet,' Gray said as he turned off the engine. 'She helped us to look after the twins when they were babies and she can't wait to see them again.'

Janet looked perfect, Holly thought, watching the woman's happy face glow pink with excitement as she waved to the children.

'Come inside where it's warm,' Janet said when they'd clambered from the car and she'd given them all, including Holly, huge hugs. 'The chill starts early on these winter afternoons, and I've got a heater on in the kitchen.'

As they followed her into the house, which was warm and fragrant with baking smells, Holly thought everything about Gray's home seemed comfortable and welcoming. Her fears, it seemed, were unwarranted.

Of course, first impressions could be deceiving. No doubt Jabiru Creek Station would soon reveal its downside. There had to be a downside. Right now Holly couldn't imagine what it might be, but something had driven Chelsea away from here.

CHAPTER SIX

THAT evening the sky put on a show, as only Outback skies could. A mass of brilliant crystal stars blazed in the vast black dome that arced from one distant horizon to the other. Gray stood on the front steps, drinking in the silence and the grandeur.

After the non-stop pace of New York, the crowds in the busy airports and the bustle of Sydney, it was good to let the tranquillity of his home seep into his veins. Since Chelsea's passing he'd been on a constant roller coaster of worry and despair, but tonight he felt calmer than he had in a long time.

Behind him, in the house, Janet was pottering about in the kitchen and he could hear the clink of cutlery and china as she stowed things away in the big pine dresser. Holly was in the bedroom down the hall, putting his children to bed, calming them after the excitement of their arrival, and the discovery of a basket of tiny three-day-old puppies in the kitchen by the stove.

Gray chuckled, remembering the shining adoration in Anna and Josh's eyes as they'd knelt by the basket, begging permission to pat the little pups that wriggled and squirmed against their mother.

Of course the children had begged to be allowed one puppy each to keep as a pet, and of course Gray had said yes, they could choose their pups as soon as their eyes were open. But no, they couldn't *both* have the all black one, and if there was any fighting neither child would have a puppy.

Holly had been a major help, backing him on this ruling and then diverting the children by offering to read them one of their favourite stories about a runaway cocker spaniel.

Already, he owed a great deal to Holly.

She'd been fabulous while they were travelling, keeping Anna and Josh entertained and comfortable, and remembering to tell them what to expect on each leg of the journey. Gray couldn't help noticing that she wasn't just capable—she was genuinely fond of his children—and he was beginning to suspect that it would be a real wrench for her to finally be parted from them.

She was quite a surprise package, actually. He'd assumed she was like Chelsea, a city girl born and bred.

Today, however, in her simple T-shirt and jeans, she'd deftly unhooked the notoriously tricky rural gate, and she'd looked every inch the country girl she'd claimed to be.

He recalled the cheeky smile she'd tossed over her shoulder when she'd told him that she'd grown up on a farm. Her dark eyes had sparkled and her lips had curled and—

'Gray.'

Holly's voice brought him swinging round.

She was standing in the doorway and she smiled shyly. 'Two little people are waiting for their goodnight kiss.'

'Right.' He spoke a little too gruffly because she'd caught him out. 'Thanks.'

He crossed the veranda to where she stood, backlit by the light spilling down the hall. Her dark eyes were shining and her pretty lips were pink and soft and wonderfully inviting…

It would be so easy, so tempting to ask his children's

nanny if she'd like a goodnight kiss, too. She was kissing close and she smelled of flowers and—

And the last thing Gray wanted was to start flirting with Chelsea's young cousin when she'd come to his home as an especially kind favour to his kids.

I must be one post short of a fence.

Relieved that he'd come to his senses in time, he strode on past Holly, down the passage to the room where Anna and Josh were waiting.

Holly lay snuggled beneath a soft, warm duvet in a pretty room that had one doorway leading to a hallway and another onto a veranda. She listened to the night sounds of the Outback, which amounted to silence mostly, punctuated by the occasional owl hoot or the soft, distant lowing of cattle. She thought how amazing it was that she could be so far from Vermont and still hear the same sounds she'd grown up with.

After the long journey she was dog-tired and tonight she'd broken the habit of a lifetime and left the book she was currently reading unopened on her nightstand. Right now, she simply wanted to take a moment, before sleep claimed her, to relive her first evening at Jabiru.

Already, to her surprise, she'd found much to like— this pleasant bedroom, for example, and its old-fashioned double bed with gorgeous brass ends, and the big homey kitchen filled with timber dressers and tempting aromas. The children's room was similar to hers, but was cheery with matching multi-coloured duvets, and Holly really liked the inviting verandas scattered with cane loungers, not to mention the cuter than cute puppies that had so enchanted the children.

She even liked the scents of grass and animals and dust that filtered in from the outdoors. She felt amazingly at home here and, despite the flight inland to Normanton and the long car journey, she found it difficult to remember she was miles and miles from anywhere. She'd expected to feel lonely and isolated, but she only had to look out of her window to see the lights of the stockmen's cottages twinkling in the darkness like friendly stars.

She thought about Chelsea and wondered how she'd felt on her first night in Gray Kidman's home. As a born and bred New Yorker, she might have found it all very strange. The children seemed to have settled in happily enough, however, although Gray wasn't as relaxed as she'd expected. Actually, there was something about him that puzzled her.

Most of the time, he had an air of quiet confidence and competence that was very reassuring. But every so often she caught a hint of his vulnerability, lying surprisingly close beneath his strong exterior. She'd glimpsed it at times when she'd least expected it—like tonight when she'd called him in to say goodnight to Anna and Josh.

Was he more worried about his new responsibilities than she'd realised? Was he scared that his children would soon grow tired of this place and want to hightail it back to New York?

Somehow, Holly didn't think that was likely and she would do her best to make sure Anna and Josh settled in smoothly but, after Chelsea's reaction to Jabiru, she could understand Gray's concern.

As she nestled more snugly under the duvet, she remembered there was one other thing about Gray that had bothered her—

His books.

Or, rather, the lack of his books.

Where were they?

As a lifelong lover of the written word, Holly had always

found herself sneaking peeks at other people's bookshelves. It wasn't so much that she was looking for books to read—this time she'd brought a good supply and she could easily order more over the Internet—but she'd always been fascinated by what books revealed about their owners—their hobbies and interests and tastes in fiction.

For her, books had always been a kind of getting-to-know-you shortcut. So far, in Gray's house, she'd seen a few recipe books and women's magazines in the kitchen, but they were obviously Janet's. Where were Gray's books?

Perhaps he was a very orderly man who liked to keep all his reading material in one place—in his study, possibly.

Yes, his study was sure to have floor-to-ceiling bookshelves. Content with that thought, she fell promptly asleep.

Holly was in the depths of sleep when the screams started, so deeply asleep, in fact, that she almost ignored them. One part of her brain urged her to respond, but she felt drugged, glued to the mattress.

But then she remembered it was Anna who was screaming.

Fighting desperate weariness, she opened one eye and saw moonlight streaming through an unfamiliar window. For a frantic moment she panicked. Where was she?

It came in a flash and she sat up, her heart thudding as she threw back the bedclothes. Shivering in the sudden cold—it was winter here, after all—she switched on her bedside lamp, shivered again when her feet met icy floorboards. Regrettably, Outback homes did not have central heating.

But there was no time to hunt for a warm dressing gown. Anna's screams had risen several decibels and she'd wake everybody in the outlying cottages. Holly dashed from her room and down the passage to the children's room.

Gray was already there. In the dark, Holly could see him sitting on the edge of Anna's bed, trying to calm her.

'Shh, Anna,' he was murmuring as he drew the little girl into his arms. 'You're okay, baby. Shh.'

Anna continued to scream.

Holly stepped closer and, although she couldn't see Gray's face, she sensed how helpless he felt. Poor man. She knew he was horrified by his daughter's terror, and tonight he was probably also worried that the screams would alarm everyone within hearing range.

Gently, Holly leaned closer and stroked Anna's hair and her soft cheek. 'Hey, Anna,' she said in her most soothing voice. 'It's okay, honey. You've had another nasty nightmare, but it's all over now. You're okay. I'm here with you, and Daddy's here, too.'

To her relief, the screams began to subside, reducing in time to shuddering sobs.

Beside her, Holly heard Gray's heavy sigh.

'It might be best if I take her back to my bed,' she offered, knowing the strange environment would make it harder for Anna to settle back to sleep this time.

Gray didn't hesitate. 'Okay. Thanks. Let me carry her for you.'

Holly nodded, then went over to Josh's bed. 'Are you okay, champ?'

'Yeah,' the boy murmured sleepily.

'I'm taking Anna through to my room, okay?'

'Okay.'

Holly gave him a reassuring hug, loving the scent of baby powder on his skin. She tucked the duvet more closely around him, then went with Gray, down the cold passage to her room. She was shivering as she climbed into bed again—was too cold, in fact, to worry about the intimacy of having Gray Kidman in a T-shirt and striped pyjama bottoms in her bedroom.

At least Anna was calmer now. She blinked in the lamplight as Gray lowered her into bed beside her.

His arms brushed Holly's arms, electrifying her, leaving her nerve endings jangling as he straightened once more and stood beside the bed.

When Holly looked up, she saw tortured darkness in his eyes.

'Anna's all right now,' she told him.

'But is she?' he whispered, unable to hide his anxiety. 'Are you sure?'

'Yes, Gray. She'll be fine. I'm sure.'

The mattress dipped as he sank onto the side of Holly's bed and she could see his hand shaking as he stroked Anna's hair. 'I'm so sorry, baby.'

He spoke in a tight voice, as if he was somehow responsible for Anna's distress. Holly had read somewhere that parenting was mostly about guilt. Looking at Gray, she could believe it.

She wanted to reassure him that he was doing a great job with his kids, but she couldn't talk about it now in front of Anna.

'You're going to sleep now, aren't you, Anna?' she said instead as the child snuggled close.

Eyes closed, Anna nodded against Holly's shoulder.

Even though the little girl was calm again, Gray continued to sit there, watching her. Holly realised she was holding her breath. He was so close she could almost feel his body heat, and he looked so impossibly gorgeous in the lamplight, so dark and manly and—

Holly caught the tropical scents of his cologne as he leaned forward and kissed his daughter.

'Goodnight, poppet.'

His blue eyes gleamed as he smiled sadly at Holly. 'Thank you,' he whispered. 'You're wonderful, Holly. Thank you so much.'

And then, before she recognised quite what was happening, he kissed her cheek.

Her entire body flared like a freshly struck match.

Gray's kiss was no more than a friendly glancing brush, but it was positioned very close to the corner of her mouth, and her libido seemed to have developed a mind of its own, creating all kinds of pleasurable expectations.

Gray straightened and stood. 'Is there anything else I can do for you? Anything you want?'

Oh, man. Holly might have laughed if she wasn't so stunned. She might have answered if she wasn't too breathless to speak. Thank heavens Anna was there, preventing her from saying anything reckless.

'I...I'm fine,' she managed, eventually. 'Anna and I will...um...both be fine now. Thank you.'

Gray stood again, looking down at them, his eyes dark once again and serious. 'Goodnight, then.' He cracked a tiny, crooked, utterly gorgeous smile. 'I hope you both sleep well.'

Holly couldn't reply, could merely nod as she watched him leave her room—watched his shiny dark hair, his broad shoulders, his perfect butt and his long legs disappear through her doorway.

'Josh?' Gray whispered into the darkness.

He heard the rustle of bedclothes and a sleepy voice.

'Is that you, Dad?'

'Yeah. I came back to make sure you're okay.'

Light spilling through the doorway from the hall showed his small son curled on his side, with the bedclothes tucked up to his chin, his longish dark hair framing his soft, fresh cheeks.

The boy was only six—so little—and yet there were times when Gray thought he caught glimpses of the man his son would one day become.

Cautiously, he sat on the edge of the bed, and the small mound beneath the bedclothes wriggled to make room for him. 'It's pretty scary when Anna screams like that, isn't it?'

Josh nodded solemnly. 'But she's getting better.' He sounded surprisingly grown-up. 'Holly says it'll stop eventually.'

'I'm sure Holly's right.' Gray was thinking of a conversation in New York when Holly had talked about his children and their grief. Ever since then, he'd felt guilty that he'd shied away from raising the subject of Chelsea's death with them.

If he took Holly's advice and talked about it more, he might be able to save Anna from her nightmares. Holly was in there now with Anna, soothing her, doing everything she could to help his daughter to feel safe…to heal.

But in a few weeks Holly would be gone, and it would be up to him. And for all he knew, Josh might need his help, too. At the moment the boy seemed to be coping just fine, but how much pain had he kept bottled up?

'Josh, I've never thanked you,' Gray began unsteadily, and already, just thinking about what he wanted to say made his eyes sting and his throat choke up. 'I've never thanked you for ringing the ambulance for your mom—'

He stopped, took a breath to clear the shake out of his voice. 'That was such smart thinking. I'm so proud of you, son.'

At first there was no sound from the bed. And then, 'But

I didn't save her.' In the darkness, Josh's voice sounded extra-tiny and quivery. 'Mommy died.'

A sob brimmed in Gray's throat and he gulped it down. 'Sometimes we can't save people, Josh.' He took a breath. 'But the big thing is, you did your best and that's so fantastic. That's why I'm so proud of you. Your mom would have been proud, too.'

Tears threatened again and the next breath Gray drew shuddered in his chest. To his surprise, he felt two wiry arms winding around his neck, and then Josh was clinging to him, his bony head pressed hard under Gray's jaw.

'Thanks, Dad.'

Gray smelled the warm just-bathed scent of his son, mingled with a faint whiff of puppy, and he was flooded with love. Then he felt hot tears wetting his T-shirt. A beat later, Josh was crying noisily, weeping as if his heart would break.

Fighting his own tears, Gray gathered the boy in and held him close, felt his small body shaking as the grief poured out of him.

Poor little kid. Gray could remember how he'd looked when he was born—tiny, red, fists curled ready to take on the world. He pictured again the fine man the boy would grow up to be.

'I'm here for you, Josh,' Gray whispered. 'I promise. I'll be the best dad ever. No matter what it takes.'

It was some time before Josh was calm again. Worn out from crying, he finally sank back onto the pillow and looked up at Gray with tear-washed eyes.

'Dad, do you think if we'd stayed here with you that Mommy wouldn't have died?'

Gray stifled a groan of dismay. His throat closed over and he couldn't speak.

'No,' he finally managed in a tight voice. 'I'm afraid it wouldn't have made any difference, mate.'

'Why didn't we stay here?'

'Didn't—' This was so hard. 'Didn't your mom explain?'

'She just said she needed to work at the ballet.'

'That's right. Your mom's work was very important to her. She was very talented and she needed to live in New York.'

Josh nodded and sighed, then rolled sleepily onto his side. To Gray's surprise, the boy was very soon asleep, his breath falling evenly and softly.

But when he went back to his own room, he lay staring at the ceiling, thinking once again about his marriage, about Chelsea, and his wonderful kids…

His old fear returned. How he could pull off being the 'best dad ever'? He wanted to be everything Anna and Josh needed, but they needed an educated father, someone who had the right connections, someone who'd learned so much more than running a cattle station.

He thought of Chelsea again, of her growing disappointment and unhappiness. He thought of his own mother, who still to this day managed to make him feel unbearably deficient.

How long would it be—years or only months—before Anna and Josh saw through his bluff and discovered the failings he'd worked so hard and so long to hide?

'Your dinner's keeping warm in the oven,' Janet told Gray two nights later, when he arrived home after a long day of shifting cattle on his western boundary. 'I've left Holly's dinner in the oven, too. Right now, she's putting the children to bed.'

'Already?' Gray glanced at the clock on the wall in surprise. It was only ten past seven. 'The kids aren't sick, are they?'

Janet laughed. 'Heavens, no. If that pair were any fitter they'd be dangerous.'

He sent Janet a cautious glance. 'How was their first day of school?'

'I'll let them tell you.'

Her enigmatic answer caused a twinge of fear—the old fear that had haunted him as long as he could remember—but Janet was smiling, so he decided he was overreacting. He set off down the hall.

Even before he reached the children's room, he heard their laughter, but then he realised the sounds were coming from Holly's room.

His pace slowed, then stopped altogether. For the past two days and nights, he'd been dealing with images of Holly in bed—which only proved he wasn't the brightest young bull in the paddock. In the midst of his poor little daughter's distress, he'd been distracted by an overpowering urge to kiss her nanny—despite the nanny's sensible flannelette pyjamas.

It was an unforeseen problem—this tendency to find his thoughts flashing to Holly. It was the last thing he'd expected, the last thing he wanted. He had no intention of setting himself up for another romantic disaster.

A burst of laughter from the bedroom was accompanied by Holly's voice, high-pitched and squeaking. Actually, the sound was more like quacking, as if Holly was acting out a story. Gray drew a bracing breath and continued on to the doorway of her room.

To his surprise, the room was in darkness. In the dim light he could see that Holly's bed had been transformed into a tent made from sheets draped from the tall brass bedposts and joined in the middle by large safety pins. The silhouettes of his giggling children and their nanny were illuminated by torchlight inside the tent.

It looked like incredible fun.

Gray stood in the darkened doorway, watching them, hands sunk in the pockets of his jeans…moved beyond reason…flooded by memories of his own lonely childhood in this house and his parents' constant bickering and battles.

Never once had he experienced anything close to this level of fun or fellowship. Later, he'd enjoyed yarns around campfires and he'd discovered the camaraderie of the stockmen in the mustering team, but his early home life had been constantly marred by his parents' tension and deep unhappiness.

By contrast, Holly was going out of her way to keep his children entertained and happy and secure. Her generosity was a revelation to him. Damn it, he was fighting tears.

Taking a deep, steadying breath, he knocked on the bedroom door.

'Who's there?' called Josh, sounding important.

'Hector Owl,' Gray responded in his most booming voice.

'Daddy!' squealed his children, and two little faces appeared from beneath the side wall of the tent.

'Hey, there. Looks like you're having fun.'

'We're putting on a puppet show.' Grinning widely, Josh lifted the sheet to reveal Holly caught in a beam of torchlight and sitting cross-legged at the bottom of the bed. Her hand was encased in a glove puppet that vaguely resembled a duck.

She blushed when she saw Gray.

'I don't want to interrupt,' he said.

Holly shook her head. 'You're not interrupting. We were only filling in time until you got home.'

'But don't let me stop your fun. Keep going.'

She smiled shyly. 'Um…well…'

'Just tell me something first,' he said, quickly. 'How was school?'

'Awesome!' his children shouted in unison.

'Really?'

Anna's eyes were almost popping with excitement. 'It's a rocket ship school, Daddy. Me and Josh and Holly are in one rocket ship and we talk on our radio to all the kids in the other rocket ships.'

'A rocket ship?' Gray shook his head in bemusement. 'Sounds exciting.'

'It is exciting. And we've already learned all kinds of math and about wombats.'

Gray smiled at Holly—seemed he wanted to smile more and more lately. 'I'll get all the details from you later.' Already he was looking forward to their conversation.

'But you'll play with us now, won't you?' demanded Josh.

'Ah…' Gray hesitated. They were probably acting out another story he'd never heard of. An excuse—an urgent need to see a man about a dog—was ready on the tip of his tongue.

'Here, Daddy,' cried Anna bossily. 'You can have a puppet.' She held up something made of bright pink fabric. 'You can be the pig.'

'The pig,' he repeated, feeling instantly inadequate, just as he had on the night Holly had pushed him to read a bedtime story.

But, despite his misgivings, he knew he *needed* to learn how to do this stuff. For his kids' sake, he had to make the most of these next few weeks while Holly was still here to show him the ropes.

'Sure,' he said, bravely walking closer to the bed and holding out his hand for the pig. 'What do I have to do?'

CHAPTER SEVEN

'So, TELL me,' said Gray after he'd heard Holly's full report on his kids' first day in their new school, 'is our Outback as bad as you expected?' He was smiling but Holly thought she detected tension in his eyes, as if her answer really mattered.

'I wasn't expecting it to be bad,' she said.

'Not even after Chelsea's warnings?'

She shook her head. 'I'm not like Chelsea,' she told him bluntly. 'Chelsea was a city girl through and through—city girl lifestyle, city girl career, city girl clothes. Not that I need to tell you that.'

They were sitting at one end of the kitchen table eating their heated-up meals. The puppet play had been a great success and Gray had joined in with gusto. Now, Janet had retired to her cottage and the children were in bed, so Holly and Gray were alone in the big silent house.

Gray had showered and changed into a fresh white shirt that made the tanned skin at his throat even darker. His hair was damp and he'd shaved, and Holly could see a small scar on his jaw she'd never noticed before. She told herself this was an everyday, average evening meal and it made no sense that she felt all fluttery every time their gazes met across the table.

'Don't you think of yourself as a city girl?' Gray asked her.

She shook her head. 'You know what they say. You can take the girl out of the farm, but you can't take the farm out of the girl.'

He smiled. 'So what kind of farm did you grow up on?'

'A dairy.'

'Really?' His eyebrows lifted with surprise. 'Dairies are hard work.'

Holly laughed. 'And your kind of farming is easy?'

'Piece of cake,' he said with a sparkle in his blue eyes that sent her hormones rattling. 'Except for when I'm driving a truck through floodwaters.'

'Or wrestling with crocodiles.'

'Yeah, or wrangling wild bulls.'

They shared another smile. Holly, trying to ignore another flutter, asked quickly, 'So how big is Jabiru Creek Station?'

'Close on a million acres.'

'Wow.' She stared at him. 'I'm sure there are countries in Europe that are smaller than that.'

Gray shrugged. 'A few, I believe.'

'But Janet told me you run this place all by yourself. She said you've been in charge here for almost ten years.'

'I have, more or less, but I couldn't have done it without the help of Ted. He's my manager and he keeps the books and looks after the paperwork. I couldn't have managed without Janet, either. She and Ted are a great backup team.'

'But you don't have any other family here?'

'No.' Gray concentrated on spearing a bean with his fork. 'As you know, my mother's in Sydney. She and my dad split up when I was a nipper. Later, my dad's health went downhill, so he moved to Cairns to be closer to doctors. But he's okay, as long as he has regular check-ups.'

Gray lifted his gaze. 'Tell me about your farm. Do your parents still run it?'

'Sure—with my eldest brother's help. He and his family live with my parents.'

'Your *eldest* brother?' Now Gray looked amused. 'So how many brothers do you have?'

'Three. All of them are older.'

Smiling, he pushed his empty plate aside and leaned back in his chair in a way that somehow made his shoulders look huge. 'So you're the only girl and the baby of the family.'

'Yes.' Holly couldn't help returning his smile. 'I know, I know. I must be a spoiled princess.'

'I can't see any signs of spoiling,' he said, letting his gaze run over her.

To her surprise, a happy kind of buzz started inside her, something she hadn't felt in a very long time. 'You haven't mentioned any brothers or sisters,' she prompted. 'Are you an only child?'

'Yeah. But I can't claim to have been spoiled.'

'No,' she agreed quietly, remembering his mother's cool reception at the airport.

Setting her knife and fork neatly together, she said, 'Actually, my brothers are my stepbrothers.'

'Really?' Gray was too well mannered to ply her with awkward questions, but she could tell he was curious. She decided she wanted to tell him.

'I've never met my real father, you see. He took off when I was a baby, so my mom was a single mom, a hairdresser, and until I was five we lived in town. Just the two of us in a little flat above her hairdressing salon. Then one day this nice guy came into her salon with three young sons who needed haircuts.'

She smiled. 'Turned out he was a lonely widower, a dairy farmer. He and my mom hit it off and, when they married, we became a family.'

To Holly's surprise, Gray frowned. 'And you've all lived happily ever after?'

'We have indeed.' Sending him a deliberately light-hearted smile, she added, 'So you know the moral of that story, don't you?'

'Do I?'

'Sure. Next time you're in town, you have to keep an eye out for a friendly but lonely hairdresser.'

It was supposed to be a joke, but she could see it had fallen flatter than Kansas.

'I'm not looking for a second wife,' Gray said grimly.

Okay. Point noted.

Holly had been thinking of her stepdad and how happy he was with her mom, how happy they both were—but perhaps she'd been insensitive. She hoped she hadn't sounded as if she was pushing Gray to find a replacement mother for his kids.

It was clear she'd upset him. Gathering up their plates, she carried them to the sink, mad with herself for spoiling a perfectly pleasant conversation. For a moment there, Gray had looked as if he wanted to pack her bags and put her on the next mail plane out of Jabiru.

Knowing a change of subject was needed, she asked, 'While I'm up, would you like a cuppa?'

'Thank you.' Already, he was sounding more conciliatory. 'I'll stack the dishwasher.'

She tried to ignore the view of him from behind as he bent over to load their plates. How could ordinary old blue jeans be so attention-grabbing?

'By the way,' she said casually as her gaze flickered to his low-slung jeans, then away. Then back again. 'I meant to thank you for letting us use your study as a schoolroom.'

'No worries.' Gray finished with the dishwasher and leaned casually against the kitchen counter, arms crossed, his eyes friendly once more. 'You're welcome to use the study.'

'It doubles really well as a school room, but I've told Anna and Josh they have to keep it tidy for you.'

He pulled a face. 'Doesn't really matter if they mess that room up. I'm not in there a lot.'

'I must admit I was surprised to find it so tidy. I thought it would be full of your books.'

Gray frowned and his eyes narrowed. 'Why?'

'Well, there are hardly any books anywhere else in the house. I thought they'd be in the study, but you obviously keep them somewhere else. I must admit I kept all mine in my bedroom in Chelsea's flat. I had them double stacked on floor-to-ceiling shelves, piled on the nightstand, on the floor—'

As Holly said this, she realised that Gray's expression had changed.

Again.

This time, however, she saw a flash of pain in his eyes. *Real* pain.

What was the matter now? What had she said wrong?

Behind her the kettle came to the boil and she whirled around quickly. Confused, embarrassed, she concentrated very carefully on pouring hot water into mugs.

When she looked back at Gray again, a cool mask had slipped over his face and his blue eyes were almost icy. 'I never have time for reading,' he said.

Okay. So here was another subject that was a conversation-stopper for this man. First, she'd upset him by asking about his former wife's preference for Sydney. Then she'd made a light-hearted comment about his marital future and hit a brick wall. Now his taste in books was a taboo topic...

Aware that the evening's lovely relaxed mood would almost certainly not revive, Holly suggested that she might take her tea through to her room and Gray looked relieved. They exchanged very polite goodnights and parted.

In bed, however, nursing her mug of hot tea, Holly couldn't help conducting a post-mortem of their conversation. She thought how much she'd enjoyed Gray's company up until the point when she'd apparently put her foot in it. Gray wasn't just a sexy dude. She'd seen glimpses of a really nice, friendly guy.

Then she'd spoiled everything. For heaven's sake, who was she to judge his reading habits? What did she know about the responsibilities involved in caring for a million acre property? Gray couldn't have been much more than twenty when he'd shouldered that responsibility, and it wasn't so remarkable that he hadn't had time to laze about with his nose in a book.

Just the same, it was clear there was more to Gray than met the eye. He might seem to be a straightforward Australian cattleman with a down-to-earth manner but, beneath the simple and sexy blue-jeans-and-riding-boots exterior, he was a complicated puzzle.

Working him out wasn't part of Holly's job description. But, if she was to leave Anna and Josh in his care, shouldn't she try to understand him?

After Holly left, Gray stayed behind in the kitchen, brooding as he stared out through the window at the dark, starless sky.

He'd been steeling himself for Holly's nosy questions.

She was, after all, a teacher but, truth to tell, her question about his books hadn't bothered him nearly as much as her suggestion about his plans for the future.

Whenever he thought about the rest of his life stretching ahead into his forties, fifties and beyond, his heart felt rimmed with ice. But was he really going to close down his emotions and never look at another woman again? Was it okay if his children never had a stepmother? Weren't Janet and a nanny enough?

He'd always looked on Chelsea's arrival in the Outback as a gift from the gods, but he'd wrecked that chance.

Had it been his only chance?

What was he planning for the rest of his life? Would he simply take advantage of casual opportunities? Or would he put himself in the marketplace—like those crazy TV shows—*Cattleman wants a Wife.*

He hadn't come to terms with any of these questions yet—and he sure as hell wished Holly hadn't raised them.

By Friday afternoon, the children were well settled into their new home. The school week had gone really well and now Anna and Josh were out of the school room and playing on the swing. It was a favourite afternoon pastime that came a close second to admiring their growing puppies, which now resembled fat little sausages with lovely seal-smooth coats.

Selections had been made and Josh was the proud pre-owner of the all black male, while Anna had settled on a sweet little blue-speckled female.

From the kitchen Holly could hear the children's voices drifting through the window, squealing with delight as they pushed the swing higher.

Janet, in the kitchen, was browning chicken pieces at the stove.

'Let me help you,' Holly said. 'Maybe I can chop something?'

Janet tried to shoo her away. 'Your job's in the school room, lovey. I don't expect you to help in here.'

'But I'd like to.' Holly was thinking of all the times she'd chopped ingredients for her mom in the pretty blue and yellow farmhouse kitchen at home. For some reason she couldn't quite explain, this afternoon she was feeling homesick.

She told herself it had nothing to do with the fact that Gray had made himself scarce all week, ever since Monday night's conversation.

'Well…' Janet took a good long look at Holly and apparently made up her mind about something. 'You could chop carrots and celery if you like. I'm making chicken cacciatore.' Then she sent Holly an unsettling wink. 'It's one of Gray's favourites.'

Hmm…Gray again…

It was surprising the number of times Janet mentioned her boss to Holly. She'd even tried to suggest that Gray was happier now that Holly had come to Jabiru Creek.

But if Gray was happier, Holly knew it was because his children were here now, and it had nothing to do with her presence. Quite the opposite. Whenever she'd talked to Gray she'd pressed the wrong buttons and upset him. Ever since Monday night he'd been avoiding her and that bothered her more than it should.

Admittedly, a cattleman needed to rise early and to be away from the house, working on his vast property from dawn until dusk. But each night, after Gray indulged in a quick after-dinner romp with his children, he took off for one of the machinery sheds, claiming he had a problem with a broken tractor.

Holly told herself that mending tractors was what men of the Outback did in the evenings instead of reading the paper, or watching TV like their city counterparts. Her father loved to tinker in his sheds, and she mightn't have minded Gray's absence so much if she hadn't been almost certain that he was dodging conversation with her.

Was he worried that she was waiting to pounce on him with more questions?

Now, at the end of a week of tractor-mending, she wished she knew if she'd said something that had really upset him, or if she was making a mountain out of a molehill. Surely her mind could be put to rest after a simple quick chat?

As she chopped carrots, she decided she would head out to that machinery shed this evening and offer Gray some kind of olive branch…

There was no helpful moonlight when Holly cautiously descended the homestead steps at half past eight, after the children were safely tucked in bed. She made her way across the paddock to the shed by the feeble glow of her flashlight.

A shadow rose from the grass beside her and large wings flapped, making her jump. With a hand pressed to her thumping chest, she thought about turning back, then told herself it was probably an owl and that crossing a paddock at Jabiru Creek was no different from playing hide-and-seek in the barns back home with her brothers.

Just the same, it felt like ages before she reached the yellow light shining through the doorway of the tall corrugated iron shed.

The sound of hammering came from inside. Or was that her heart?

A few more steps brought her through the doorway and inside the shed. She saw rubber tyres of all sizes stacked against a wall. Bits and pieces of rusty machinery. An intact tractor.

Gray—not in the expected overalls, but in his usual faded jeans and an old navy-blue woollen sweater with the sleeves pushed back and a hole at one elbow—was working at a long wooden bench. He'd stopped hammering now and was planing timber, smoothing down the edges of a very large box-shaped object.

Intent on his task, Gray turned slightly and Holly saw the strength in his hands and forearms. She could even sense the movement of his shoulder muscles beneath the thick wool of his sweater.

She turned off her flashlight and put it in her coat pocket. Her palms were sweaty, so she jammed them in her pockets too. Then, feeling like an intruder, she took a deep breath and went three steps deeper into the shed.

She felt ridiculously nervous. Any minute now Gray would look up and she would have to explain why she was here.

She tried to remember the opening she'd rehearsed. *Something about his tractor.* But he wasn't working on the tractor...

With her gaze firmly fixed on Gray, she took another step forward—and tripped on a metal pipe, sending it rolling and clattering across the concrete floor.

Gray's head snapped up and his blue eyes widened with surprise. 'Holly.'

'I'm sorry,' she cried, bending down to rub her smarting ankle.

'Are you okay?'

'Yes, I'm fine.'

He came hurrying over to her, wiping his dusty hands on an old rag. 'Are you sure you're all right?'

'The pipe's probably worse off than I am. It's okay. Really. Just a bump.'

'I hope you don't end up with a bruise.' A beat later, he said, 'What are you doing out here?' His smile was quickly replaced by a frown. 'Is something wrong? Is it Anna?'

'No, no. Nothing wrong. A-Anna's fine.' Holly's mouth was suddenly as dry as the sawdust on the floor. She tried to swallow, then remembered that she'd planned to smile to set the right mood. 'There's no problem, Gray. The children are sound asleep.'

'That's good to hear.' With hands on his hips, he studied her, a puzzled gleam lurking in his bright blue eyes. 'So, what brings you out here at this time of night? I thought you'd be curled up with your nose in a book.'

Yes...well...

Now that he was waiting for her answer, Holly felt more foolish than ever. Gray seemed totally relaxed and not at all put out by her sudden appearance, so how could she suggest there was a problem that needed sorting?

'Have...have you finished the tractor?' she asked.

'The tractor?'

'I...um...thought you were working on one.'

'Oh, yes. You've blown my cover.' Gray's eyes twinkled, and then he turned to the bench where he'd been working. 'I've been making something for Anna and Josh, actually. It's almost done.'

'Oh,' she said in a very small voice.

'Would you like to take a look? I still have to paint it.'

Without waiting for her answer, Gray went back to the bench and picked up the large boxlike frame he'd been working on. Not quite hiding his pride in his workmanship, he set it on the floor.

'Oh,' Holly said again when she saw it properly. 'It's...
it's a puppet theatre.'

He was grinning. 'I made the stage high enough for
Anna and Josh to stand behind.'

'It's perfect.' Holly meant it. She was amazed and she
felt so silly for thinking he'd been avoiding her. She wasn't
even on his radar.

'They'll love it,' she said. 'Wow. You've even made a
pointy roof and a little wooden flag to go on top.'

'And Janet's making red velvet curtains.'

'Fantastic!'

So Janet was in on this, too? Holly felt as if the rug had
been pulled from beneath her. Here she'd been, all week,
stewing about Gray's sensitive reaction to their conversation, while he'd been busy creating a wonderful surprise
for his children.

'It's a fabulous idea,' she said, running her hand over
the smooth silky wall of the stage and admiring the fine
craftsmanship. 'Did you say you're going to paint this?'

'I thought the kids would like something bright.' He
scratched at the side of his neck. 'But don't ask me about
colour schemes. Apart from painting the roof red, I'm a
bit stumped.'

'You can't just nip down to a hardware store, so I suppose it depends on what paint you already have.'

'Practically every colour under the sun, actually.' He
went over to a cupboard against the wall and flipped it
open to reveal several shelves lined with spray cans. 'Last
year there was a ringer working here who moonlighted as
a rodeo clown and I helped him to make his props.'

Holly laughed. 'So you have enough colours to make a
rainbow.'

'I guess I do.'

'Rainbow walls would be fiddly, but they'd look fab-ulous.'

Gray considered this, a smile pulling at a corner of his mouth. 'I'm no Vincent Van Gogh.' He shot her an amused glance. 'What about you? Are you handy with a spray can?'

Holly had wielded many a spray can while making children's library displays, and she'd discovered a creative streak she hadn't previously known she possessed.

'We—I mean *you*—would need to work from the top down,' she said. 'And you'd have to use something like cardboard as a shield.'

'You'd help me, wouldn't you?'

She knew she shouldn't feel so flattered. 'I'd be prepared to give it a go.'

'Terrific,' he said, matching her enthusiasm.

And then, looking straight into her eyes, he smiled. *Oh, man.* His smile packed a wallop.

Not that she should be noticing.

It shouldn't have been so much fun—working hard and staying up till nearly midnight to get the last rainbow stripe in place. Holly enjoyed every second of the project.

Early in the evening, while the undercoat was drying, Gray boiled a billy on a small gas ring and made tea. He had milk and sugar in a battered old cooler and even a packet of cookies.

They sat on rickety camping stools in the middle of the messy shed, drinking sweet hot tea from chipped enamel mugs and eating cookies.

'Yum,' Holly said as she helped herself to a second one.

'Good to see a girl with an appetite.' Gray took a second

cookie as well. 'Chelsea was always so careful about what she ate.'

'All dancers seem to diet. They're very strong-willed,' she suggested.

'Obsessed,' Gray said tightly.

Holly now knew better than to pursue this sensitive topic. After all, she'd come here to hold out an olive branch.

Smiling, she said brightly, 'So tell me, Gray, does your hat still fit?'

He looked at her with puzzled amusement. 'Last time I tried it. Why?'

'Janet and Ted have both been praising you to the skies this week and I thought you might have a swelled head.'

Looking down at the curls of shaved wood on the floor, he shrugged. 'That pair are biased.'

'Maybe, but they're not easily hoodwinked. They told me you're a brilliant cattleman, highly respected and looked up to by others in your industry. Ted said that when you took over the reins here ten years ago, you dramatically improved the carrying capacity and diversified the cattle breeds. And you placed yourself at the cutting edge of land management and water conservation.'

Gray was staring hard at his mug. 'Sounds a bit grand when you put it like that, but when I'm out, driving around, I listen to a lot of agricultural radio programmes. It's a good way to learn things.'

'According to Ted, you hoard all that info in your brilliant memory and then put it into practice.' Holly smiled. 'He also said you're fantastic with figures. He called you a human calculator.'

Gray shrugged again. 'That man has far too much to say. I'm not paying him to gasbag.' His eyes flashed a cheeky challenge. 'And why are you trying to flatter me?'

'I'm not flattering you. I'm giving you positive feedback. You can blame my teacher training.'

'Yeah, right.' He gave a smiling shake of his head. 'But shouldn't we be working out how we're going to paint these rainbow walls?'

They decided on a plan. They would start at the top with orange just beneath the red roof, then progress downwards through blue and purple to finish with green at the base.

With the plan settled and the undercoat dry, they got back to work. After a short trial run, Gray admitted that Holly could produce the most even spray paint finish, so they agreed that he should hold up the cardboard shield for her.

As they worked, she engaged him in safe topics—mostly about the twins and their first week of school. She told him that Josh was very clever at arithmetic and had developed a passion for Natural Science—particularly frogs.

'I hope you don't mind. This afternoon we converted a pickle jar into a tadpole aquarium,' she told him.

Gray laughed. 'I was mad about spiders when I was a kid. Tried to start a redback spider farm in an ice cream container.'

'Eeeeww.' Holly gave an elaborate shudder, then told him that Anna was the twin who was curious about spiders. 'She also has beautiful handwriting and a musical ear and an exceptionally vivid imagination.'

Holly enjoyed herself immensely, which surprised her, considering that once upon a time she'd looked forward to sharing this sort of task with Brandon. She'd even been silly enough to imagine that she and Brandon would paint a nursery for their first baby, and she'd actually picked out a colour scheme of white and sunshiny yellow with a brightly coloured rainbow frieze.

How strange that this puppet theatre inspired her now almost as much as her old dream had.

On Sunday morning, Gray rose just as the screeching corellas took off from the trees along the creek bank, and he crossed the frosty grass to the shed where the puppet theatre stood in all its rainbow-walled, red-curtained glory.

He grinned when he saw it. It looked so bright and cheerful and, even if he did say so himself, very professional. Almost as good as the puppet theatre he and Holly had taken the children to see in New York.

His kids were going to love it.

All thanks to Holly, of course...

Without her, he wouldn't have known such things existed. And without Holly he wouldn't have enjoyed the final decorating tasks nearly as much. She was so easy-going and comfortable to be with.

Gray totally understood why his kids loved school when Holly was around to help make it fun.

How would they cope when she left?

Soon, he would have to seek her help in posting an ad for a replacement nanny, and then he'd also need her input when he vetted the applicants.

Right now, Gray couldn't think of a more unpalatable task, couldn't imagine another woman filling Holly O'Mara's shoes.

A movie director couldn't have created a more pleasing scene than Anna and Josh's discovery of the puppet theatre. They bounced into the kitchen for breakfast, spied the theatre positioned just outside the flyscreen door, and reacted just as Holly had hoped they would—with dancing and squealing and their eyes almost popping out of their heads with excitement.

'And it isn't even our birthday,' Josh exclaimed in grinning disbelief as he and Anna took turns to pull the cord that drew the splendid red curtains open and shut.

Anna was beaming, too. 'I can't believe we have a theatre *and* our puppies. Wow, Daddy, this is so cool.'

Together, the children squeezed inside the 'back door' and examined the stage. When they plied Gray and Holly with questions, they were stunned to learn that their dad had actually made this glorious construction with his own hands.

Holly smiled at Gray, taking in the quiet satisfaction in his eyes.

'They'll remember this day for the rest of their lives,' she told him quietly.

He merely nodded, but this time when he smiled back at her, she had to look down. The crackling *something* in the air was suddenly too much.

After breakfast, the children jumped straight into presenting their premiere puppet show on the veranda, and of course Holly, Gray and Janet were the audience, very happy to sit on a row of chairs, with the basket of puppies at their feet.

'The puppies have to watch, too,' Anna had insisted.

Naturally, the show was received with thunderous applause, and afterwards the children rushed straight off to plan their next performance.

'We'll soon be calling them Shake and Speare,' Janet muttered good-humouredly, before she returned to the kitchen to make a batch of scones for morning tea.

Holly might have followed Janet if Gray hadn't detained her with his hand on her arm. She jumped at his touch as if he'd burned her, and then she felt seriously foolish.

'Would you like to come for a drive with me?' he asked.

'A drive?' She needed a moment to catch her breath. 'I'm sure we won't be able to prise Anna and Josh away from their puppets.'

The tanned skin around his blue eyes crinkled. 'I wasn't planning to invite the children. I'm sure they'd rather stay here, and they'll be fine with Janet.'

'But—' Holly's heart gave a strange thump. 'Are you sure Janet doesn't have other plans?'

'I'm certain of it, Holly. I've already spoken to her, and she'd love to spend a day with the twins. In fact, she's already started on a picnic lunch for us.'

'Oh? I…I see.'

'You've earned a day off, and I thought you might like to see the gorge.'

It was kind of Gray to take the trouble to entertain her. 'Thank you.' Holly's voice was a shade too proper and polite. 'I'd love to see the gorge. I'll explain to Anna and Josh—'

He held up a hand. 'I can do the explaining while you get ready. You'll need sunscreen and a hat and sturdy shoes.'

She was being bulldozed—steamrollered—but for once she didn't mind.

In her room, as she grabbed her shady hat from its hook on the back of her dresser, she caught sight of her reflection in the mirror. She was, as usual, in a boring old T-shirt and jeans, with her hair tied back and a new crop of freckles on her nose.

If she was in New York, she was quite sure that if a new man invited her out for the day she would go to a great deal of trouble, hunting through her wardrobe for the perfect outfit, ringing her friends for fashion advice, going for a manicure, a pedicure, a leg wax.

It was strange to think that she was now going to spend an entire day alone with a man who was *not* Brandon, and yet she didn't feel an overwhelming urge to worry about how she looked. It was rather comforting to know she didn't have to try too hard with Gray Kidman.

After teaming with him on the puppet theatre, they'd reached a comfortable working relationship and she could save her dating charms for the new man she was bound to meet once she was back home again in the fall. The sizzle she felt around Gray Kidman was nothing more than hormones—and she supposed she should be grateful to know they were still in working order.

CHAPTER EIGHT

As Gray drove away from the homestead with a cloud of dust pluming behind his vehicle, Holly was reacquainted with how very isolated Jabiru Creek Station really was.

They'd only just passed the last outbuilding before they were once again following a faint dirt track across endless plains that stretched and stretched to the distant horizon. She saw nothing but cloudless blue skies, red dirt and dusty faded grass, with occasional mobs of silvery hump-backed cattle sheltering in the scant shade of straggly white-trunked trees.

'It must be fabulous to tear across this country on horse-back,' she said, partly because she meant it, and partly because she wanted to say something positive about the monotonous scenery.

Gray turned to her, clearly surprised. 'Do you ride?'

'I haven't for ages.'

'But you know how to.'

'Sure. There was a time when horse-riding was my favourite sport.'

His eyebrows shot high. 'Why didn't you tell me?'

'I came here to be your children's nanny. Not to prance around on horseback.'

Still watching the track ahead, Gray shook his head.

'But I'm sure you could squeeze in a little riding time while you're here.'

'That would be wonderful—although I'm sure I'd be sorry when I was stiff and sore.'

His eyes sparkled as he turned to her. 'You'll soon loosen up.' A little later he said, 'I'm planning to teach Anna and Josh how to ride.'

'Oh, good. They'll love it.'

'Even Anna?'

'Especially Anna,' Holly assured him. 'She's getting more into life in the Outback every day.'

Gray smiled. 'I'll have to measure them up for riding helmets.'

After that, he seemed to lapse back into thoughtful silence, and Holly sensed his focus shift from conversation to the ancient landscape all around him.

Eventually, a red range of hills appeared, rising out of the flat land ahead of them. Holly was reminded of the backdrops of the old western movies her dad used to watch on Sunday afternoons, and she almost expected to see smoke signals puffing from the jagged ridges.

When they crested a hill, Gray braked and in front of them the land dropped away, plunging, without warning, down sheer red cliffs.

'Oh, my gosh!' Holly was glad of her seatbelt. Leaning as far forward as the belt would permit, she peered through the dusty windscreen. 'I guess this must be the gorge?'

'It's not quite the Grand Canyon.'

'But it's spectacular.' She glanced back over her shoulder to the rear window and the view of the empty plains they'd just crossed. 'Are we still on your land?'

'Sure.' Already Gray was opening the driver's door. 'Come and take a look. I love it out here.'

Outside, the sun was scorching hot. Holly jammed her

hat firmly on her head, but she wasn't keen to step any closer to the edge of the gorge. It was an awfully long way down to the glinting water of the rock pools at the bottom. After just a hasty glance down there she felt dizzy.

'Here, come with me.' Gray had retrieved their backpacks from the rear of the truck and he handed the smaller one to Holly. 'I'll show you the best way to see the view.'

She almost declined. She had quite a nice view from where she was standing, and she had a safe hold on the truck's sturdy metal bull bar, thank you very much. But Gray was holding out his hand to her, and his air of confidence was very convincing.

Summoning her courage, she managed to loosen her grip on the bull bar and his hand holding hers felt wonderfully strong and trustworthy, but she clung to him so tightly she was afraid she'd leave bruises.

To her relief, he led her away from the cliff's edge to what at first seemed like a hole in the ground, but turned out to be a man-made staircase cleverly hewn out of the rock.

'This leads down through the roof of a cave,' he said.

'Wow. Did you make these stairs?'

Gray laughed. 'No way. They've been here for over a hundred years, but my grandfather helped to carve them out.'

Intrigued, Holly allowed him to guide her down the rocky staircase. Already she could see that the cave below them wasn't gloomy or dark, but filled with sunlight. And it had a wide sandy floor, so she began to feel calmer.

By the time they reached the bottom of the steps, she looked around with amazed delight. The cave was set into the side of the escarpment and it formed a safe shelf, a fabulous, cosy viewing platform offering a spectacular view all the way down the gorge.

'Gray, it…it's fabulous.'

His blue eyes met hers, watching her closely, as if he was intensely interested in her reaction. Apparently satisfied, he smiled. 'Not bad, is it?'

'It's amazing. I think I'll sit down though, so I can take it all in.'

By this time, she'd become super-aware of their linked hands—of the heat of Gray's palm against hers, of the pressure of his fingers as he gripped her firmly and safely. To her surprise, she was incredibly reluctant to release his hand before she lowered herself to the sandy floor.

Once she was seated, Gray edged forward, closer to the mouth of the cave, and he hunkered down, taking in the view. He loved this place with its rock pools that reflected the sky and the spectacular sandstone escarpments carved out of the ancient landscape. He never failed to be moved by its grandeur.

But today he was trying to imagine how the gorge might look through Holly's eyes. He wasn't sure why it mattered so much, but he found himself hoping that she might somehow understand what it meant to him.

At least she wasn't talking non-stop. She seemed happy enough to drink in the atmosphere, or to quietly take photographs with her small digital camera.

In the languid silence Gray let his shoulders relax against a warm wall of sandstone. He heard the warbling notes of a pied butcherbird and a flock of galahs calling in the distance. Below, on the water, a pair of grebes floated.

After a while, he asked quietly, 'So, what do you reckon?'

'This is so beautiful,' Holly said softly. 'It feels almost… spiritual.'

A good answer. 'It *is* spiritual,' he said. 'At least it is for the Aborigines.'

And for me, he added silently, thinking of the many times when his life had hit rock bottom and he'd come to this place to search for some kind of peace.

Moving carefully on her hands and knees, Holly crawled a little closer, then sat cross-legged, looking out. 'It's awesome. Unforgettable.' She spoke in a hushed undertone, the way people talked in church.

She took a few more photos, then lowered her camera. 'I'm sure this gorge has been here for ever. A dinosaur could come lumbering out from behind a rock and it wouldn't look out of place.'

Her face was soft, her dark eyes luminous with wonder. And Gray had to look away, concentrating his attention on a lizard as it disappeared down a crack in a rust-stained rock.

He'd hoped Holly would like this place, but he hadn't expected her to so totally *get* its timeless mystery.

'Is it weird to feel that there's someone here?' she asked. 'A gentle spirit, looking after us?'

He had to swallow the hard lump in his throat before he could speak. 'Not weird at all. That's why I love it. Sitting here quietly, taking in the silence, always makes me feel stronger. Uplifted. The Aborigines call it "listening to country".'

He turned and saw Holly nodding slowly, a pretty smile lighting her eyes.

'Listening to country,' she repeated softly. 'I like that. I used to do a lot of that when I was growing up in Vermont. On my way to school I used to love walking over the covered bridge on Staple's Brook and along the banks beneath sugar maples and birches. *Listening to country.* I am so on that page.'

Launching to his feet, Gray moved to the very mouth of the cave, appalled to realise he'd been on the brink of tears. He'd never expected to meet a woman like Holly, someone lovely and sweet and in tune with his world. For a heady moment there, he'd almost pulled her close and kissed her, tasted her smile, her laughter.

Not a bright idea. She was here to help his children, and she was going home to America to start a fancy new job. Besides, she'd just had her heart broken by some fool of a boyfriend. Last thing she needed was her cousin's Australian ex making a move on her. Especially as that ex was absolutely useless at making women happy—or keeping them happy, at any rate.

For all kinds of reasons, he'd be a fool to start anything with Holly. Even if she did claim to love his Outback, he couldn't expect her to want to stay here. Not with him. She'd soon realise her mistake, just as his wife had.

Hell. He should wear a danger sign, warning women to keep their distance.

'This country must inspire musicians and artists,' Holly was saying. 'Or writers. I've never read any literature about your Outback, but there must be novels and poetry. Do you have any—?'

She stopped in mid-sentence and her face turned bright red, as if she realised she'd made a dreadful gaffe. 'Sorry. I know reading's not your thing.'

Gray's entire body tensed, as if the cliff had suddenly crumbled away beneath his feet. Fear knifed through him— the fear of ridicule that he'd never managed to shake off.

His only hope was to change the subject...

'I could give you a few lines of bush poetry,' he said quickly.

Anything, even the embarrassment of a recitation, was better than risking exposure of his incompetence.

'Poetry?' Holly sounded shocked, and already he was feeling foolish.

She was leaning forward now, hands wrapped around bent knees. 'Gray, I'd love to hear some bush poetry.'

Of course he was already regretting the offer. He wasn't a performer and he wished he could come up with an excuse—he'd forgotten the lines—anything. 'It's pretty basic stuff. Hardly Wordsworth or Shakespeare.'

'But the simplest things are often the truest.'

Damn. Gray knew he'd talked himself into a corner. He'd look even more foolish if he backed out now. He made a show of clearing his throat and then, keeping his gaze fixed on the gorge, he began to recite.

'I've crossed harsh country parched and red,
With ghost gums shining white,
Where sand dunes choke the river bed,
And all day I prayed for night.
I've heard that country sing to me
In the stillness of my mind,
A Dreamtime chant from rock and tree—'

Gray paused and he realised that Holly was staring at him, her eyes full of questions.

'Sorry.' He could feel his face burning. Why the hell had he grabbed onto the poem to get him off the hook?

'Don't apologise. I loved it, Gray.'

He shrugged elaborately and looked away again, down the gorge to where a mob of black-tailed rock wallabies were feeding quietly on the moist vegetation at the edge of a waterhole.

'When did you learn that poem?' she asked, with the nosiness he should have expected from a teacher.

Gray shrugged. 'Can't remember.'

'Who wrote it?'

The heat in his face deepened and he answered

brusquely, without looking at her. 'It's nothing. Just something I made up.'

He heard her shocked gasp. 'You made it up?'

'Yeah. No big deal.'

'But...when did you write it?'

He gave another big-shouldered shrug. 'Years ago. I can't really remember. Beside a campfire. Sitting here. Alone.' Sure that his face was crimson now, he got to his feet and scooped up his backpack, eager to be done with this conversation.

'Gray, please don't be embarrassed, but it *is* a big deal that you've made up such a lovely poem. I'm seriously impressed.'

'Thanks.'

'Did Chelsea love it?'

Chelsea? He sighed, then stared out at the deep blue of the sky and the deeper red walls.

'I shared my poetry with her once, but she saw it as yet another excuse to plead with me to give up my cattle and head for the city. She wanted us to be artists together—she could be a choreographer in Sydney and I could perform my poetry.'

'That doesn't sound very...practical.'

'She was convinced I'd be a great hit. She was always looking for something else for me to do besides raising cattle.'

Holly made no comment, but she was frowning and then, as if she'd been struck by a bright idea, she flipped open her backpack and pulled out a notebook. 'I'd like to write your poem down.'

'Why?' Still thinking about Chelsea, Gray growled the word suspiciously.

'Because it's great. I really like it. I want to be able to read it again later, when I'm back in America.'

Already, she was sitting with her small spiral notebook in her lap, open at a blank page, her pen poised, ready to write.

Gray forced himself to relax. There was no threat in Holly's request. He actually liked the idea of her taking out her notebook when she was back in busy, bustling Manhattan, turning to his poem...reading it... Maybe she'd recall this moment. This peace.

Where was the harm in that?

Feeling self-conscious but no longer uncomfortable, he began to recite again: 'I've crossed harsh country parched and red...'

Holly's pen flew across the page leaving a neat curving script in its wake.

'With ghost gums shining white...'

She nodded enthusiastically as he continued on to the end of the first verse, then added a second stanza.

'Wow, that's fabulous,' she said when he'd finished. 'Thank you.' She spoke warmly, and her cheeks were flushed and her dark eyes were suspiciously shiny as she slipped the notebook back into the pack and closed the flap.

'You're welcome.'

'Having a copy of your poem makes this trip to the gorge even more perfect.'

He was more pleased than he should have been, but he was determined not to show it. Poker-faced, he said, 'So... would you like to keep going all the way to the bottom of the gorge?'

'Sure.' Holly scrambled to her feet and accepted his hand with almost childlike trust. 'Lead the way.'

Gripping Gray's hand once more as they made their way carefully down the rough, steep track to the bottom of the gorge, Holly discovered she was in deep, oh-my-God trouble.

She'd learned two important things about Gray just now—his soul-deep love of his land, and a strong reason for the breakdown of his marriage.

And then she'd learned something about herself.

While she'd sat in the cave in the middle of Gray's shatteringly beautiful wilderness, listening to him shyly recite his poetry, something huge had happened, something totally unexpected, something guaranteed to break her heart.

The noonday sun reached deep into the gorge, warming the wide ledge of rocks where they ate their simple picnic of egg and lettuce sandwiches on homemade bread, along with doorstop slices of rich fruity cake, and oranges.

Holly leaned down, dipping her fingers into water so clear she could see tiny silvery fish feeding on the sandy bottom.

Gray was busy lighting a fire for their billy tea and he called to her, 'Is the water cold?'

'Cool, but not freezing.'

'We could go for a swim if you weren't afraid of crocodiles.'

'Well, of course I'm afraid of crocodiles. Who wouldn't be?'

Catching his grin, she knew he'd only been teasing.

She sat up to watch him work, to watch the smooth tanned skin on the back of his neck and the damp line of sweat on his collar, the stretch of his cotton shirt over his wide shoulders, his long fingers deftly snapping twigs and poking them into the flames.

She imagined changing into bathers and swimming with him—if there were no crocodiles—and sweet shivers ran through her.

'The billy will take a few minutes to boil.' Gray's voice broke into her musings. 'We may as well make a start on our tucker.'

Holly discovered, to her surprise that she was ravenous and the sandwiches were surprisingly fresh with just the right balance of mayonnaise and pepper.

The gorge was completely silent now. Earlier there'd been bird calls but, in the midday stillness, the birds had retreated. Gray, looking very relaxed, sat with his back against a warm rock wall, his long jeans-clad legs stretched in front of him, his face shaded by his broad-brimmed hat.

Holly was quite prepared to eat her lunch in silence, lazing like a lizard in the sun and growing drowsy. And she was sure that was what Gray wanted, too, so she was surprised when he spoke suddenly.

'So...what made you decide to become a teacher?'

'Oh, that's easy,' she said. 'I was inspired by my fourth grade teacher, Miss Porter. She was lovely and brilliant and kind. And she turned our whole class onto books and reading.'

Gray nodded slowly, watching her from beneath his shady brim.

'I started out as a regular classroom teacher in Vermont,' Holly explained. 'That was fine for a few years, but all the time I was in the classroom I could feel the library calling to me, so I decided to get extra qualifications to run school libraries. That's when I moved to New York.'

'And you left your boyfriend behind.'

'Yes.' Holly waited for the slug of pain that always hit her when she thought about Brandon. It eventually came, like a delayed reaction, and it still hurt but, to her surprise, it was no longer crippling.

She realised that Gray was watching her, but he swiftly

switched his gaze to the fire and the boiling billy and he lifted it from the fire, then added tea leaves and gave them a stir.

'Are you ready for your tea?' he asked after a few minutes.

'Thank you.' Gratefully, Holly accepted an enamel mug of tea that was black and sweet and hot. Sipping it helped to calm the strange new tension inside her—a tension that had nothing to do with talking about Brandon and everything to do with her present company.

'Gray—'

'Hmm?' He leaned comfortably back against the rock and sipped his tea.

'Did you have School of the Air when you were a child?'

'Do you *have* to start talking about school right now?'

'I don't suppose it's essential, but I just told you about my favourite teacher. And I was thinking about your lovely poem, and I wondered where you learned about poetry.'

'It certainly wasn't on School of the Air.'

'Did you go away to boarding school?'

This was greeted by a deep sigh. 'Can we give this a miss, Holly?'

'I'm a teacher. I can't help wanting to know these things.'

'School is not everyone's favourite subject.'

'Is this another conversation stopper?'

He frowned. 'What do you mean?'

'It seems to me that every time I have a conversation with you I run into trouble. There's always something you don't want to talk about. Chelsea, I can understand. But what's wrong with talking about school?'

'The school a person went to doesn't matter out here in the bush. We're not snobs about that sort of thing.'

'I'm not asking you to show off. I was just curious—*anything* about your school would do. Best teacher, worst teacher. Favourite subject, favourite sport—'

There was a movement on the rock beside her. A beat later, Gray was close beside her, leaning in to her, and Holly realised with a shock that he was planning to kiss her.

Small explosions detonated all over her body.

She was sure she should say something to him, but her brain refused to cooperate.

When Gray touched his lips to hers, her surprise melted like sugar in hot tea and—*oh, man*—she responded like a person in a dream.

His mouth was like the sun burning across the sky, moving over her mouth, inch by fiery inch, cautious at first, and testing. Holly remained perfectly still, afraid that at any moment she might wake up and feel obliged to behave responsibly.

She didn't want to behave responsibly. She was too curious initially and then she was bewitched by his totally masculine enchantment.

Already, she was melting, softening and, when her lips drifted apart, Gray accepted her invitation without hesitation. His hands cradled her head and his kiss, tasting faintly of orange and tea, became clever and darkly seductive.

She could smell the sunlight on his skin, could feel its warmth on her closed eyelids, and she was sinking beneath it. Melting beneath his persuasive lips. Melting and needy. So needy. She could no longer resist him even if she'd wanted to.

A sweet, compelling ache started low inside her, urging her to lean into him, to link her hands behind his neck and to return his kiss, to communicate with her body the shocking, thrilling impatience that had taken possession.

Oh, heavens, she might die if he stopped.

A sound broke the noonday silence—half a whimper, half a moan. Amazingly, it had come from her, but she couldn't stop to worry about decorum now.

But, to her dismay, Gray pulled away from her.

'Holly.'

Noooo. She kept her eyes tightly closed.

In the stillness she could hear the hammering of her heartbeats and the reckless pace of Gray's breathing.

He dropped a soft kiss on the bridge of her nose, then moved further away.

'What—?' she began, then had to pause to catch her breath.

His sexy blue eyes were apologetic. 'I'm sorry,' he said.

Sorry?

Oh, God. How could he share the hottest kiss of her life, possibly the most fabulous kiss since the beginning of time, and then apologise as if it were a mistake?

Distraught, Holly stared at him. 'Why are you sorry?'

'I shouldn't have done that.' His throat rippled as he swallowed. 'Please don't read too much into it.'

'But why did you do it? Why did you kiss me?'

He offered her a rueful smile. 'It seemed like a good idea at the time.'

'You kissed me to shut me up?'

Gray merely shook his head and Holly sank back against the rock in dismay.

What a klutz she was.

She'd gone into swoon mode, allowing herself to be completely carried away, while Gray had merely found a new technique to stop her from asking nosy questions.

'I'm an idiot,' she said out loud.

'No, Holly.'

'What am I, then?'

His answer was a smiling shake of his head. 'Another question? I should've known it's dangerous to kiss a teacher.'

'Yes, you might learn something,' she snapped, but her response was even testier than she'd intended. She'd never been any good at jokes, and light-heartedness was doubly impossible when she was so upset.

Damn Gray. She could still feel the warm pressure of his lips on hers. She could still smell him and taste him, could still feel the ripples of pleasure pooling low and deep inside her, like aftershocks.

But for Gray the kiss had been a game, a purely practical ploy to stop yet another annoying conversation.

Not daring to look at him, Holly jumped up quickly and, in a bid to cover up her embarrassment, she began to tidy away their picnic things.

As they took the climb back to the top in easy stages, Gray was uncomfortably aware that he'd spoiled a perfect day. He'd let Holly think that he'd kissed her to distract her and, yes, it was true. More or less. She'd pushed their conversation in a direction he had no wish to follow. She'd been holding his feet to the fire of a secret shame and he'd had to stop her.

It was a bad habit that had started during his marriage. Whenever his wife had come up with one of her grand schemes for getting them away from Jabiru Creek, he'd found it easier to seduce her than to tell her the truth—that he had no employable skills beyond running this cattle property.

But, although his initial impulse to kiss Holly had been self-preservation, everything had changed the instant their lips had touched.

A kind of spell had come over him. Admittedly, it was way too long since he'd kissed a woman, so that might explain why he'd been so totally fired up. But abstinence couldn't explain why he'd felt emotionally connected to Holly, or why there was so much that felt *right* about kissing her, so much that felt right about just being with her.

In spite of her nosy questions, she was amazingly easy company, and she was surprisingly at home here in his Outback. He found himself wanting a deeper connection with her, and his body still throbbed with a need to lose himself in her sweet, willing embrace.

It was a lucky thing that her soft needy cry had brought him to his senses. Without that warning, he might never have found the willpower to stop. But now he'd hurt Holly by once again going into defensive mode. He'd protected himself, but he'd spoiled something special.

Damn it, he should have known better.

Hadn't his marriage taught him that he was no match for a clever, educated woman, no matter how strong her appeal? Hadn't his life lessons proved that he was better on his own?

He was fine on his own.

Or at least he would be until his kids' education caught up with him.

The journey back to the homestead was wrapped in uncomfortable silence, which meant Holly had plenty of time to brood as they rumbled across the trackless plains.

She thought about the moment, while she and Gray were looking down at the gorge, when she'd experienced a feeling of true connection with him. In the same moment, she'd realised something else—she hadn't wanted to fall for Gray but it had happened, almost against her will.

Which meant he had the power to hurt her, just as Brandon had.

She shouldn't have allowed him to kiss her. Why hadn't

she shown more sense? Here she was—still suffering from shell shock after Brandon's dumping—and the last thing she wanted was another romantic entanglement—especially with Chelsea's ex.

She wanted freedom, not complications. Why would she put her heart at risk when she had a fabulous job lined up to go home to?

Please don't read too much into it he'd said.

How could Gray kiss her into oblivion simply to shut her up? What was his problem? Where was the crime in asking him about his school? Or about his lack of books, for that matter.

He knew schools and books were her thing, and just because—

Oh, my God.

A sudden chill skittered down Holly's spine as all sorts of puzzling things about Gray suddenly started to fall into place.

The lack of books in the Jabiru homestead. The fact that he'd never heard of Winnie-the-Pooh. His reaction in New York when she'd suggested he should read to his children. The way he'd waved away menus, and brushed aside the Central Park pamphlet—

Could he have literacy problems?

She stole a glance at him now…at the snug stretch of denim over his thighs to his strong, sun-weathered profile.

Gray Kidman…expert cattleman, gorgeous, take charge of anything…

Surely he couldn't be illiterate?

It was hard to take in.

But if he'd grown up out here, miles away from schools and possibly without a tutor, it wasn't too much of a stretch to believe that he might never have learned to read. He

probably knew a few words that enabled him to function—
Departures and Arrivals in airports, for example—but
beyond that—

Holly remembered his mother's lack of warmth. What
had her role been in her son's early years? Had the tension between them started decades ago? Holly knew from
her teacher training that literacy problems often stemmed
from emotional issues connected to early schooling
experiences.

She also knew that illiterate people could still be incredibly astute and competent—and Gray was clearly intelligent
and gifted. He made up poetry in his head. How many
people did that? With Ted's bookkeeping help, he managed
his business very successfully.

Her soft heart ached to think that a proud and capable
man like Gray could have a problem he'd felt compelled
to hide, managing superbly in spite of it.

Then again, she might be overreacting—jumping to
totally incorrect conclusions.

The last of the daylight was turning the paddocks to
pink and mauve as they pulled up outside the homestead.
Crickets and katydids were already singing their dusk
chorus in the trees by the creek.

Anna and Josh, freshly bathed and in their dressing
gowns and slippers, came running down the front steps to
greet Holly and Gray, while Janet hurried after them like
a fussy mother hen.

'They've been no trouble,' Janet assured Gray. 'They've
been busy in the school room for most of the day.'

'I thought they'd be playing with their puppets,' he
said.

'The puppets have had a good airing, but mostly they've
been doing their homework.'

'Homework?' Holly frowned. 'But I didn't set any homework.'

'Well, they've been beavering away on some kind of writing project for the puppet house.' Janet laughed. 'I'm definitely renaming them Shake and Speare.'

'We're going to have a puppet show after dinner,' Anna explained with great excitement. 'And there's a part for everyone.'

Out of the deep pockets of her cherry-red dressing gown, she pulled folded sheets of paper and, glowing with pride, the little girl separated three pages for Holly, three for Janet and three for Gray.

Each sheet was covered in photocopies of her best printing.

'You're Hector Owl, Daddy, and I'm Timothy Mouse and Josh—'

Holly didn't hear the rest. She was too busy watching Gray and the dawning horror in his eyes.

Her heart galloped as she looked down at the paper in her hand. Clever little Anna had written a rudimentary play script with a list of characters and lines of dialogue beside the characters' names.

It was the sort of creative writing exercise the twins had been encouraged to try at their progressive school in Manhattan, and Holly wanted to be thrilled for them. She *was* thrilled, actually, but she was also very worried about Gray.

Were her suspicions about his literacy correct? Was this his personal D-Day?

Judging by the sudden paleness of his complexion and the unhappy twist of his mouth as he stared at the paper, the answer was…

Yes.

Her heart broke for him as she watched him force a crooked smile.

'Wow,' he said. 'A play. Aren't you two clever?'

'You have to put on your growliest voice,' Josh informed him.

'I see.' Gray tapped the paper and blew out his cheeks thoughtfully. 'So have you changed much of my original story?'

'We've changed lots!' exclaimed Anna. 'See!' She pointed importantly to her script. 'You can read it all here. We've made up a whole new story, so we can have the owl and the mouse, as well as a frog and a wombat and a pig. There are parts for everyone.'

Gray looked decidedly ill.

CHAPTER NINE

GRAY looked down at the script in his hand, fighting hot panic. It was covered in Anna's childish, clever printing and, as always, he could catch a word here or there, but then the letters of all the other words blurred. He couldn't breathe. His heartbeats hammered in his ears.

I've got to get a grip. I can't lose it now.

As casually as he could manage, he said, 'But you can't have a puppet play without puppets and you don't have an owl puppet, do you? I'll have to make one before you put on the show.'

'No need, Dad,' said Josh. 'Janet's already made us an owl. She's made it out of a tea cosy.'

Gray was very familiar with the brown and yellow knitted cosy that Janet used to keep the breakfast teapot warm, and he could imagine how easily it would have converted into a perfect owl puppet.

'Your play sounds very exciting,' Holly told the children in her best kind-but-firm nanny voice. 'But, right now, your father and I need to collect our picnic things from the truck and put them away, and then we have to get cleaned up for dinner.'

Grateful for her intervention, Gray turned back to the vehicle to fetch their backpacks. To his surprise, Holly came with him.

'Organise a phone call,' she said cryptically out of the corner of her mouth.

'A phone call?'

'Yes.' Her gaze was very steady, her dark eyes huge and shining with determination. 'If one of your friends calls you straight after dinner—an important business call that you have to take in your study—you'll miss the puppet play, but the twins will get over their disappointment.'

Gray stared at her, stunned.

Holly smiled gently and placed her hand on his wrist. 'Janet and I will play puppets with Anna and Josh. We'll send them to bed happy.'

Oh, God, Holly *knew*.

She knew everything.

Gray's throat tightened on a razor-sharp knot of shame.

Holly knew. She'd guessed the weakness that hurt him so deeply he couldn't even bring himself to name it in his private thoughts.

Today he'd kissed her in a desperate bid to stop her from talking about it. Now he was in danger of being exposed in front of his children and he didn't deserve Holly's help, but she was offering him a lifeline.

'You're right,' he said, resisting an urge to sweep her into his arms. 'A phone call's a good option. Thank you.'

He spoke more gruffly than he'd meant to. Then he slammed the door on the back of the vehicle and swung his pack over one shoulder.

He couldn't look at Holly as they walked back into the homestead together. It was hard to accept that the shame he'd successfully covered up for more than twenty years was finally out in the open. Right now, he couldn't bear to see Holly's lovely eyes brimming with sympathy.

He felt like such a fraud. This evening Holly was saving

his bacon, but what would happen tomorrow and the day after that? He couldn't keep hiding the truth from his children. The fate he'd always feared had now arrived, and he had no choice but to brace himself for humiliation.

Around eight-thirty, Holly tapped on the door to Gray's study.

'Who is it?' he called cautiously.

'It's Holly.'

'Come on in. The door's not locked.'

When she pushed the door open she found him sitting at his desk in a pool of lamplight. He rose stiffly from the chair, giving the surprising impression that he'd aged in the hour and a half since dinner. He had a sad and caved-in air, as if he'd received a terrible blow.

'Are the children in bed?' he asked.

'Yes, all tucked in.'

'Are they happy?'

'As pigs in mud.' Deliberately, Holly smiled as if nothing was wrong. 'They were disappointed you couldn't join them in the fun, but they understood about the phone call.'

'Thank you.' He spoke with almost formal politeness.

She felt compelled to warn him. 'Anna and Josh are treating this evening's performance as a dress rehearsal.'

'Right.' Gray's mouth twisted in a wry attempt at a smile. 'So they still plan to have a grand performance?'

'I'm afraid so. With a full cast, including the hero, Hector Owl.'

His mouth tilted again, faintly. 'When? Tomorrow night?'

'That's what they're hoping.'

He nodded glumly and looked so unhappy Holly was moved to the edge of tears.

'Don't worry, Gray,' she said quickly. 'I can help you with this. I'm actually quite good at this sort of problem.'

He shook his head. 'I'm quite sure you're a brilliant teacher, but—'

'Before you say *but,* take a look at this.' She pulled a folded sheet of paper from the pocket of her jeans and, as she handed the sheet to him, she drew a deep breath, hoping it would calm her. She was almost as nervous as he was.

Gray unfolded the sheet and swept a brief glance down the page. His mouth tightened. 'What is this?' His blue gaze flicked to her, flinty with anger and despair.

'It's your poem, Gray. I've printed it out for you.'

'My poem?' His eyes flashed disbelief, but then he looked down at the page again.

Holly held her breath as she watched him—the formidable, proud cattleman standing in the middle of his study, with photographs of prize bulls on the wall behind him and a shelf full of silver trophies that he'd won for campdrafting.

Now, with his shoulders braced, boots planted firmly on the Oriental rug, he was frowning at the sheet of paper with deep concentration...

And then...she saw his lips begin to move as he followed the words across the page, sounding out each familiar syllable beneath his breath.

I've...crossed...harsh...country...parched...and... red...

Her throat stung to see this big, capable man reduced to small boy vulnerability. She swallowed and blinked madly, not daring to shed tears in front of him.

He continued on until he reached the bottom of the page. When he finished, he looked up, a dazed kind of hope shining in his eyes.

His throat worked and deep colour stained his cheekbones. 'I'm sorry. I should have offered you a seat.' He indicated the sofa against the wall, deep and inviting with plump vermillion and green striped cushions. 'Please, sit down, Holly.'

As she obeyed him, he returned to the chair at his desk and, almost immediately, as if he couldn't resist it, he began to read his poem again.

When he finished he looked up. 'So...how does this work? Is it like a code? If I become familiar with these words, do you think I can use them to decipher all the others?'

'That's one of the tools you can use,' Holly said. 'As for the puppets, I can easily go through the play with you, and we can rehearse your lines the way actors do. It's not exactly a three-act Shakespearean drama. Anna and Josh probably won't even notice if you ad-lib the odd line here and there.'

Gray nodded slowly, then pulled out the sheets of the play script from a drawer in his desk. A tiny spark shone in his eyes and he sent her a playful wink.

'Okay, teacher. I'm game if you're game.'

He came and sat on the sofa beside her.

It was fun—way too much fun, really. Holly loved every minute of sitting with Gray, trying to ignore the tingles his proximity caused as she read through the script with him.

It didn't take long for him to get the gist of the simple little story and his character's role, and only a little longer to learn his lines. He had an excellent, well exercised memory.

Afterwards, they sat in the late night silence, basking in a warm sense of accomplishment.

'Anna's so clever, isn't she?' Gray said, looking down at the script with bemusement.

'She's your daughter, Gray.'

'She's her mother's daughter. Chelsea was clever and creative.'

'And so are you.'

As she said this, she saw the shutters come down on his face.

'It's true,' Holly insisted. 'You're every bit as clever as Chelsea, or your children. You're missing one skill set—that's all—and I think I can help you with that.'

With a groan, he launched to his feet. Holly jumped up beside him. 'I'd be sorry to see you run away from this again.'

He sent her a sharp glance, piercing, almost venomous.

Holly stood her ground. 'You've learned your lines tonight and you'll get through the play tomorrow with flying colours. But what about all the times after that? You know there'll be more challenges.'

'I'll manage.'

'Yes, you will. You've managed very well for a long time, but you'd manage so much better if you could read and write.'

There. She'd brought the harsh truth out into the open.

A terrible sound broke from Gray as if something inside him had fractured. His face contorted with pain and Holly felt her heart stand still. The tears she'd been holding back spilled down her cheeks.

This was *so* hard for him. She had said out loud the words he couldn't bear—that he couldn't read or write.

Had she been too cruel?

She'd only spoken up because she was sure she could help him. If she was strong enough—if they were both strong enough—she could get him through this. And then he'd be free...

Savagely swiping away her tears, she reached out and touched Gray's arm.

'Why don't we just talk about it?' she said gently.

He answered with a groaning sigh.

But Holly wasn't prepared to give up. 'I'm guessing that something happened when you were little. Can you tell me?'

He shook his head. 'What's the point?'

'It could be important. I know you're intelligent and exceedingly capable, which means there's probably an emotional reason why you didn't learn to read. Have you ever talked to anyone about this?'

'No.'

'Not even with Chelsea?'

He shook his head.

Holly wasn't surprised. She'd often suspected that her cousin had fallen in love with Gray's gorgeous looks, but had been unable to meet his deeper needs. Which meant he'd carried this burden alone for too long.

'I'm no shrink,' she admitted. 'But I think talking about it might be the first step.'

'Talking? You want me to lie down on the couch and talk about my childhood?' He stared at her, jaw stubbornly jutting forward.

Holly held her breath, and waited. Then, to her relief, she saw a glimmer of a smile.

'All right, Dr O'Mara. I may as well give it a shot.'

Gray didn't actually *lie* on the couch, but they both made themselves comfortable. He poured them both a Scotch, which Holly wasn't used to drinking but, to be companionable, she sat nursing her glass.

Gray took a gulp from his glass. 'Okay—where do you think I should start?'

'Did anyone ever begin to teach you to read?'

Gray sighed. 'My mother tried.'

Holly remembered the woman she'd met at Sydney Airport and the obvious tension she'd sensed between mother and son. 'Was she living here with you at Jabiru?'

'Yes. We had the lessons—if you could call them lessons—right here in this room. I hated it,' Gray said. 'I loved my mother, of course, but I used to dread our reading sessions.'

'Why?'

'I knew they were a chore for her, and she was always impatient. I used to panic, trying too hard to please her, but then I'd be slow and she'd get frustrated, and she'd end up in tears.'

Oh, Gray. Holly hated to think of that poor little boy trying to please his difficult mother and failing dismally.

Gray downed the second half of his Scotch and set the glass aside. 'It didn't help that my mother hated living out here. She and my dad had terrible rows almost all the time. They were heading for divorce, although I didn't realise it. Then my reading—or rather my lack of it—became a huge issue during their pre-divorce wrangling. My mother blamed my father. He blamed her.'

'They argued about your reading in front of you?'

'Sometimes,' he said bleakly. 'But even when they were behind closed doors, I could still hear their raised voices. I felt so guilty. I was the cause of all their unhappiness. I knew if I could read they'd love each other again and everything would be okay. But my mother had already washed her hands of me.'

He stood and went to pour another drink, then changed his mind and came and sat beside her again. 'No point in getting sloshed over something that happened years ago.'

'You can have mine if you like.' Holly held up her

glass. 'I've only had a few sips. I'm not much of a Scotch drinker.'

He took it with a watery smile. 'Thanks.' After a sip, he said, 'You're right. I think it does help to talk about this. I've never really allowed myself to think about it.'

'I can see how the reading broke down,' she told him. 'You developed an emotional block about it.'

'My writing was just as bad. The crunch came just before my mother left Jabiru. I wanted to beg her to stay and I thought if I wrote her a letter and told her how much I loved her that of course she'd stay. No question.'

He forced a bitter laugh, but Holly could hear the terrible pain in it. She wanted to pull that hurt little boy into her arms, to hold him and comfort him.

'The letter was going to be a wonderful surprise for her,' Gray went on. 'I slipped it under her bedroom door. Worst mistake of my life. My parents had the ugliest fight over my spelling.'

Slumping back against the cushions, he closed his eyes. 'They were yelling and I heard every word. She said my letter was illegible. I was hopeless. Unteachable. A disgrace.'

Holly shuddered, but she could so easily imagine the note full of spelling mistakes. Shaky printing. Almost no punctuation. And yet it would have been a message straight from the heart of a distraught little boy. How could Gray's parents have ignored that?

'It sounds as if your mother couldn't cope,' she said. 'But surely your dad stood up for you?'

Gray shook his head. 'That was the other side of the problem. My old man never had much faith in book learnin'. That's what he called it. He hadn't had much schooling and most of his mates hadn't, either, and he reckoned they were okay. Who needed Will-bloody-Shakespeare and

encyclopaedias? Books couldn't help a man to catch a wild
bull, or strain fencing wire.'

Holly nodded, imagining the situation—the stubborn,
uneducated cattleman married to the tense, unhappy city
woman. In the next generation, history had repeated itself
in Gray's marriage to Chelsea.

'Did your mother leave?' she asked.

Gray let out another hefty sigh. 'It happened a few days
later. She left us and went to live in Sydney, and it wasn't
long before she found a new husband. A property developer.
Their son went to the best schools, and now he's a bright
young investment banker.'

'And you stayed here with your father?'

He nodded. 'My education was purely practical from
then on.' From beneath lowered lids, Gray sent her a lazy,
lopsided smile.

Holly shivered as a wave of longing washed through
her. When he looked at her like that, she could only think
about snuggling up to him and running her fingers over his
skin. She clenched her hands tightly to stop herself from
reaching out to touch him.

'So,' she said primly, 'you didn't have a nanny, but what
about School of the Air?'

Gray shook his head.

'You mean you had no schooling?'

'That's…the story, I'm afraid.'

'But how could your father get away with that? Surely
there must have been someone in the Education Department
asking questions about you?'

'Probably.' His shoulders shifted in a shrug. 'I think
my dad made sure I was away with the mustering team
whenever anyone official came snooping around asking
nosy questions. He prided himself on teaching me practical
skills and keeping me clear of books and schools. When

I look back, I can't help thinking he kept me away from books as a reaction to Mom leaving us.'

But that's a crime! Holly wanted to shout, but she bit down on the words. Criticising Gray's father was not going to help him now.

'By the time I was old enough to understand what a handicap I had, it was more or less too late, and by then I was also too proud and stubborn.' He gave another shrug. 'As I said, I've managed.'

'You've managed brilliantly.'

'I made sure I knew how to write my name and my address, and how to fill in basic forms. If I'd really wanted to, I might have found a way to teach myself more. But I never really needed reading in my line of work. And now—' He paused and frowned at the glass in his hands.

'I'm guessing that you'd rather Anna and Josh didn't have to know too much about your lack of schooling.'

He stared at the glass. He hadn't finished drinking it, but he set it aside. Very quietly, he said, 'I can't go on hiding it from them. And I'm sure it's too late for me to start learning now.'

'I don't think so.' Holly spoke just as softly as he had. Then, because she couldn't help herself, she leaned closer and kissed his cheek. 'In fact…I'm quite sure it's not too late.'

Their faces were only inches apart. She could see his individual eyelashes and the tiny flecks of grey floating in the blue of his irises. She felt her skin grow hot.

Her words *I'm quite sure it's not too late…* seemed to hang in the air. It was almost as if she was no longer talking about reading. Gray was looking at her with a burning intensity that stole her breath.

It would be so easy to lean closer still, to fall into his

arms and invite a repeat of their kiss. She wanted nothing more.

But somehow she found the strength to move away. She had to think clearly. She had to remember that the kiss at the gorge had not been prompted by Gray's desire for her. He'd made that quite clear. The important thing now was to remember that she only had a few weeks left in Australia and she had to at least make a start in teaching him to read.

She would never forgive herself if she didn't try.

'Actually, it's probably too late to start reading lessons tonight,' she said, keeping her eyes lowered. 'But we could certainly try for tomorrow night—once the children are in bed.'

Then she looked up, she saw the shimmering emotion in Gray's eyes. He lifted a hand, as if he was going to touch her hair. She felt a hot flame rush over her skin, then he seemed to think better of it and he let his hand fall.

'Thank you,' he said simply.

'You're welcome.'

'I mean it, Holly. Thank you so much. You're an amazing girl. You have no idea—'

'But I do,' she said. 'I have a very good idea.' She forced a small smile. 'That's why I'd really like to help you.'

He grinned, looking suddenly younger, lighter, freer. 'You've done so much for me. What can I do for you in return?'

Kiss me again? Good grief, where was her common sense? 'Maybe you could organise some riding practice?' she said quickly, grasping at straws. 'Not just for me, for the kids as well.'

'I will. First thing in the morning.'

Gray sat for ages after Holly left, looking around at the four walls of his study and replaying the memories he'd bared to her. To his surprise, the unhappy recollections were already losing their power to hurt him. It was as if talking about his memories, setting them before Holly—Exhibit A, Exhibit B—had made them real, no longer private nightmares, but clues in a crime.

At some deep level, he'd always believed that the not-reading business was his fault. He'd let Chelsea walk away from him because he'd always known that he wasn't really worthy of her. But the reality was: his mother had stuffed up teaching him to read. His father had held him back from a decent education.

Okay, his dad had taught him almost everything he knew about cattle and engines and carpentry, but the world was a big and complicated place and homespun knowledge only took a man so far.

For the first time Gray felt entitled to accept that he wasn't totally to blame for his inadequacies. Then again, it *was* his fault that he'd done nothing about the problem he'd been left with. Hell, if he'd had a physical handicap, he would have sought medical help; he certainly wouldn't have tried to cover it up.

Then again, it was true that practical skills were highly valued in the Outback. In a way his dad was right. You didn't need book-learning to ride a fleet-footed horse or to clear heavy bullocks out of the scrub, or to sell and buy cattle at an auction.

But, in the scheme of things, the Outback was a limited world and he wanted his kids to have choices he'd never had. Choices meant education.

Holly would never know how much it had cost him to admit to her that he couldn't read or write. Hell, he still flinched just saying the words 'read and write' in his head. But, thanks to her, the words no longer made him feel sick and hopeless. With her help, he was finally going to do something about it.

He felt like a man who'd been let out of jail.

He should tell Holly that some time. It would probably make her smile, and he really liked—no, he downright *loved*—to see her smile.

'Now it's Holly's turn,' Gray told his children. 'She's going to show us how a farm girl from Vermont mounts a horse.'

He'd woken them all early, declaring it was time to start riding lessons before school, and he'd brought four of his gentlest horses into the home paddock. Already, Anna and Josh were smugly sitting astride small, quiet ponies, while Gray held their reins.

Holly had hoped to get in a little riding practice without an audience, but now three pairs of eyes were watching her first attempt.

She shot them a warning frown. 'I told you it's a long time since I've been on a horse.'

'But you won't have forgotten how,' Gray assured her.

'My muscles might have forgotten.'

He grinned. 'That's defeatist talk.'

Holly knew he was probably right, and perhaps it was her attitude that brought about her problems for, no matter how hard she tried, she could *not* swing her right leg up over the saddle. After the umpteenth embarrassing try, she felt like a ninety-year-old former ballet dancer who'd insisted she could still do an arabesque.

'Here, let me help you,' Gray said, handing the reins to his children and instructing them not to move till he returned.

'I'm sure I'll get the hang of it—' Holly insisted as she began to lift her leg one more time.

Then she felt Gray's hands on her bottom. With a firm shove, he hefted her high and suddenly she was up in the air and she swung easily into the saddle.

Anna and Josh cheered.

'Thank you,' she said, but when she looked down into the smile in Gray's eyes, her breath caught. His eyes were shimmering with a special light.

Just for her.

Small fires flared in the pit of her stomach. She could still feel the warm imprint of his hands on her behind and now she was remembering the way he'd kissed her at the gorge. She was almost certain that he was remembering it, too. She'd always thought that he'd kissed her to shut her up. Now she wasn't so sure...

The atmosphere in the study that evening was different right from the start.

Gray was in high spirits after the puppet play. Anna and Josh had been thrilled with his Hector Owl rendition, which wasn't surprising considering how heartily he'd thrown himself into the role.

The children had been overexcited, actually, and they'd taken a while to settle to sleep, but all was quiet now. Janet had retired to her cottage for the night, and Holly had joined Gray in his study.

He could hardly wait to get started on the reading lessons and his eyes were shining. 'Take a look at this.'

From a drawer in his desk he produced a manila folder, letting small squares of paper flutter from it onto the desk's surface.

Holly picked up a square and turned it over to find the word 'red'.

'I recognise that printing. It's mine. Did you cut it out of your poem?'

Gray grinned. 'I photocopied the poem, then cut out all the words.' He looked incredibly proud of himself, exactly the way Anna had looked when she'd produced her play script. 'Choose any word,' he said. 'Test me to see how many I know.'

Holly hesitated. She wanted to ask if he'd had enough time to learn all these words. There were rather a lot of them, after all, but if she showed any sign of doubt, she would undermine his confidence.

'It's okay,' he said, sensing her hesitation. 'I've been practising out in the shed all afternoon.'

'Wow. That's conscientious.' She picked up a piece of paper and handed it to him.

'Dreamtime,' he said, smiling broadly. She tried another word and another and he knew them, too.

Holly grinned at him, thrilled for him, knowing how pleased he was. 'I knew you were brilliant.'

And suddenly his arms were around her and she was being squeezed against his big broad chest, and then they were dancing a crazy jig, bumping into the desk and knocking over a chair and not caring two hoots.

Breathless with laughter, they finally collapsed onto the sofa, panting and grinning stupidly. Holly was quite sure she'd never felt happier, or more uplifted and exultant.

Or more in lust.

Then Gray went very still and everything changed as the air became electrified with tension.

His tension and hers.

'Holly,' he whispered, trailing his fingers down the side of her neck to her collarbone.

She tried to reply but no sound came out. She was too aware of his body pressing against her, too aware of his arousal, and of her own desire coiling and tugging low inside her.

Heat flooded her. She struggled to ignore it. This shouldn't be happening. Wasn't she supposed to be still in love with Brandon, still pining after Brandon...?

She was super-aware of how different Gray was from her ex-boyfriend—he was a bigger, more muscular man, darker, more intense. Everything was different...the feel of his skin beneath her fingers...his breath on her neck...

And ever since he'd kissed her yesterday she'd been aching for more...

Even though he'd tried to dismiss the kiss as a mistake, she'd been yearning for the heady closeness of his lips locked with hers, of his arms about her, of his strength binding her...

She longed for his touch...couldn't bear it if he turned her away now.

'Please don't tell me this is wrong,' she whispered.

'Holly, I wouldn't dare.'

It was all the permission either of them needed. His lips grazed her cheek, then he kissed his way to her mouth... first taking her lower lip and drawing the soft flesh between his teeth in wonderfully intimate possession.

He was an expert, she realised gratefully, and already she was kissing him back. Indeed, she couldn't stop kissing him.

As she wriggled beneath him, positioning herself against his hardness, she heard his groan and, when he touched his tongue to hers, their kiss turned wild.

Moments later, they were helping each other out of their clothing.

CHAPTER TEN

THE next morning there was school and Holly was grateful for the routine of breakfast, bed-making and setting up the school room. Gray had already breakfasted and left before she and the children woke, so she didn't have to worry about catching his eye across the kitchen table.

That was a good thing. If he'd been there, she might have found herself blushing—and who could blame her after the sexy moves they'd made on each other last night?

Now she had a whole day to compose herself, and to convince herself that last night had been a celebration, but nothing more. They had both been thrilled about Gray's breakthrough, and then they'd experienced a kind of romantic movie moment, when they'd been a little carried away.

Well, okay, more than a little carried away.

Nevertheless, it was time to remind herself that Gray wasn't looking for a serious relationship. Last night had probably only happened because she was the only young woman within a hundred kilometre radius.

For her part, she'd decided that making love with Gray had been a necessary step in her post-Brandon recovery plan. A healing tonic.

At least, that was what she tried to tell herself, but as soon as she'd woken this morning she'd wanted to dwell on every amorous and blissful detail of Gray's lovemaking, wanted to savour his sweet tenderness and his breathtaking passion.

But now she had to put a lid on those memories. It was time to put these last few weeks with Gray and his children into perspective.

In a month's time—maybe less than that—a new and permanent Australian nanny would arrive, and that woman would occupy the teacher's seat in Gray's study. That woman would join in the puppet plays and that woman would, no doubt, be taken to admire the beautiful gorge. She might even go horse-riding with Gray and the children.

Holly's future lay in America—in a new city and a new school. All kinds of opportunities were bound to open up for her there. Maybe even a new man.

Why couldn't she feel happier?

'I think we should agree that last night was a one-off, don't you?'

Holly had been practising this suggestion all day and, now that she and Gray were alone in his study for another reading session, she was relieved to get it out in the open—especially as the sizzle between them was even more obvious than it had been last night.

'I mean,' she said now, feeling obliged to explain her point, 'we both know we could never have anything more than a fling, and flings are—'

'Fun?' Gray suggested with a smile that was hard to read.

'I was going to say dangerous.' Holly sat primly away from him on the sofa with her arms and her legs crossed. 'I'm your children's nanny, after all.'

'That's true,' he said, in a tone that suggested this wasn't a convincing argument.

'We have to think of Anna and Josh,' she added quickly before she tossed prudence out of the window. 'It could be disastrous if they cottoned onto any…um…liaison between us.'

'I guess you're right.' This time Gray sighed, then reached for her hand and gave it a gentle squeeze. 'Damn it. I suppose teachers are always sensible and right.'

Feeling the warm pressure of his fingers, Holly was overwhelmed by a need to throw herself into his arms. One more time.

Heavens, she was a hypocrite. Now that Gray was agreeing with her, she felt disappointed. Truth was, she'd never experienced such exciting, heart-thumping sex, hadn't known she had it in her to be so passionate.

Now, she had to forget her newly enhanced libido and she had to remember why she'd started this conversation.

'Children can't be expected to understand casual relationships. It's not healthy for them—and after everything Anna and Josh have been through—'

Gray nodded and then he frowned. 'I wish I knew what to say. Thank you sounds crass. But I have so much to thank you for, Holly.'

His smile was both sad and cute as he lifted a strand of her hair and tucked it behind her ear. 'Last night was amazing and special and unforgettable. We shouldn't look on it as a mistake.' His eyes shimmered and his throat rippled. 'We need to be friends for a long, long time.'

'Yes.' It was little more than a whisper.

'But what you're doing for my kids is more important than anything.'

Determined not to cry, she spoke without looking at

him. 'My job now is to prepare Anna and Josh for their new nanny.'

She was relieved that Gray agreed. Really, she was, or at least she would be once she was back home and safely embarked on her new career.

The question of the replacement nanny came to a head two weeks later.

The day started on a high note when the mail plane landed on the dirt airstrip with its load of newspapers, letters, catalogues and packages.

Like everyone else at Jabiru Creek, Holly looked forward to the weekly mail delivery. It was a major social event and Gray, Holly and the children piled into the truck to go down to the airstrip to chat with George, the mailman, and any passengers he might have brought with him 'for the ride'.

Sometimes George had time to come back to the homestead for a cuppa and a gossipy chat, but this week he was in a hurry, with engine parts needed urgently by their neighbours at Half Moon Station.

Holly grabbed a moment for a quick word with George about an idea she'd had for a book exchange between the women she'd met via School of the Air. He thought this was a great idea and promised to spread the word.

Back in the homestead kitchen, they opened their mail. There were the usual bills and letters to be handed over to Ted, as well as books Holly had ordered over the Internet— for herself, for the children, and now, discreetly, adult literacy books for Gray as well. He was making fantastic progress.

This week there was also an unexpected package.

'What's this?' Anna cried. 'It's got your name on

it, Holly.' She gave the parcel a squeeze. 'It feels like clothes.'

'Clothes?' Holly looked up with a frown. 'I haven't ordered any clothes.'

She saw a hasty, almost smug look flash between Gray and Janet.

What was going on?

With a little shove, Anna sent the parcel sliding over the table to Holly. 'Open it,' the little girl urged with a giggle of excitement.

'I don't know if I should. It might be a mistake.' Holly gave the package a tentative squeeze. It certainly felt like clothing. She double-checked the address. It was definitely addressed to her. 'This is weird.' She checked the postmark. 'It's from Melbourne.'

'They have lovely dress shops in Melbourne,' Janet remarked, staring rather fixedly at the teapot.

'I'm sure there are very nice dress stores in Melbourne, but I didn't—'

'Oh, go on and open the thing.' Gray was almost scowling at her. At least he was trying to scowl, but his eyes betrayed an ambiguous, half-amused glint. 'It's obviously for you.'

It seemed silly to hesitate any longer. 'Can someone pass me the scissors?'

Josh was closest to the old ginger jar on the kitchen dresser, where scissors, wooden spoons and other utensils were kept. Like most boys, he wasn't interested in clothing but, after he'd delivered the scissors, he hung around Holly's chair to watch her cut through the thick tape.

Everyone in the room was watching Holly, especially Gray. Her heartbeats picked up speed.

'It's wrapped in beautiful tissue paper and looks like

it must be terribly expensive,' she said as she opened the padded envelope.

She shot a shocked look Janet's way. About ten days ago, right here in this kitchen, she and Janet had been poring over catalogues together. They'd decided to order riding gear for the twins and, once that was organised, they'd idly thumbed through the women's fashion pages and Holly had gone into a swoon over the most beautiful cocktail dress.

It had just been a bit of fun. Holly had never spent exorbitant amounts of money on her clothes. Chelsea was the one who'd been fashion mad, while Holly had lashed out on books.

'Hurry up and open it.' Josh gave Holly's elbow a nudge and she opened the tissue-wrapped parcel carefully, trying not to tear the fine pearl-grey paper.

All eyes were on her.

And, suddenly, the last layer was lifted and there it was— the beautiful red wool crepe dress from the catalogue.

Holly couldn't speak. She was stunned. She shot a questioning glance to Janet, who lifted her hands in a don't-ask-me gesture and nodded her head towards Gray.

'Do you like it?' Gray asked, frowning.

'It's gorgeous,' she could only whisper.

'Hold it up,' Anna demanded. 'We want to see it properly.'

Holly pushed her chair back so she had room to stand, then displayed the dress by holding it against her. It was divine. The wool crepe was so soft and refined, the finishing was superb and the colour was strong but not gaudy.

'That red is perfect with your dark hair,' Janet confirmed.

'It looks like it should fit you.' Gray spoke casually enough, but he was watching Holly with a breath-robbing intensity.

'It does seem to be my size,' Holly agreed, checking the label. 'But…but I don't understand.'

'It's a thank you present.' From across the table, Gray's eyes gleamed. 'From all of us.'

'Oh.'

Her spirits soared for a beat and then, just as quickly, the wind dropped out of her sails. It was silly to be suddenly upset, but it occurred to her that a thank you present was more or less the same as a farewell present. Everyone here was quite calmly preparing to wave her goodbye.

Holly, on the other hand, was finding it harder and harder to think about leaving here. She loved these people. More than ever now, Anna and Josh felt like her own children, Janet was fast becoming a close friend, and Gray—well, her feelings for him were in a league of their own. But everyone at Jabiru Creek was very dear to her.

To her horror, she was struggling not to cry. How silly. They weren't about to give her marching orders.

'Thank you,' she finally managed to say. 'Thank you so much. I've never had such a lovely dress.'

'You should try it on,' Anna urged.

'Now?'

'Wear it for us tonight,' Janet suggested. 'I'll cook something special for dinner and we'll eat it in the dining room.'

'And I'll put on a tie,' Gray added with a smiling wink.

'Wow! A party!' Anna clapped her hands. 'A new dress party.'

'I guess that's better than a farewell party.' Holly couldn't help it. The comment just slipped out.

It was met by a circle of such puzzled glances that she wondered if she was reading too much into this.

She went back to her room and hung the dress on a padded hanger in her wardrobe and decided that yes, she'd

probably been jumping to conclusions about the significance of this gift. It was just a kind thought. Not a clear
goodbye.

After all, there was still almost a month before she was
due back in the United States.

One thing was certain: she was not wearing this elegant
dress to dinner without first spending time on her groom-
ing. She would have loved to rush out to the nearest beauty
spa to be professionally made over from head to toe but, as
that wasn't an option, she retired to the bathroom as soon
as the children were released from the school room.

A shampoo and blow-dry, a manicure, a pedicure and a
DIY leg wax—*ouch*—were all on the agenda. Holly spent
ages over each task, wanting to be as close to perfect as the
beautiful dress deserved.

She chose her best uplift bra and her barely-there pant-
ies and, when at last she was ready, she tried the dress on
in front of the long oval mirror on her wardrobe door and
she…was…

Gobsmacked.

Wow. Was the vision in the mirror really her?

She turned left and right, spun around to check out the
back view. The dress was divinely cut with a deep V neck-
line and had no sleeves and an elegant side tie. The colour
made her complexion glow and the fitted bodice and slim
skirt gave her more noticeable curves and a glamour she'd
never dreamed of. Even her hair looked more glamorous
than usual—extra glossy and dark and bouncy.

Thrills of excitement tingled all over her. What would
Gray think of his lovely gift now?

When Gray came home that evening he sensed a general air
of excitement in the homestead. Delicious aromas wafted
from the kitchen and from the dining room there came the

tinkle of silver and glassware as Janet set the table with the best dinnerware. From the children's bathroom came the sound of taps running.

In his bedroom, he was surprised to discover that his housekeeper had taken the trouble to lay out clothes for him—well pressed moleskin trousers, a crisp pale blue shirt and his best navy-blue and silver tie.

It was clear Janet wanted this evening to be a big success. She was very fond of Holly and she'd taken a great delight in helping him to think of the right gift for her.

'That dress is perfect,' Janet had said. 'It's something Holly would never think to buy for herself.'

Gray had been worried that Holly wouldn't like something so...so dressy. He'd only ever seen her in the simplest of T-shirts and jeans. Her taste in clothes was almost the opposite of Chelsea's. His former wife had always wanted her clothing to be that little bit different from everyone else's, with one shoulder bared, or keyholes cut in the back, or frills where you least expected them.

Holly's simple styles suited her calm, warm spirit—the spirit and sense for which he was so increasingly grateful. Of course she'd been right to stop their affair before it had barely started.

It nearly drove him crazy to spend each evening working with her on his reading instead of making slow, languorous love to her. But he was grateful—or, rather, he was *amazed* at the progress he'd made. With Holly, reading had become an exciting challenge instead of a black art to be feared.

He'd wanted to thank her and Janet had convinced him that the dress was the answer.

'Holly spent ages looking at it in the catalogue,' Janet had assured him. 'And it's not frilly or fancy. It's a classic look. She'll knock your eyes out when you see her in it. Just you wait and see.'

At the time he'd almost imagined that his housekeeper was trying to matchmake, but why would she bother? She knew as well as he did that Holly would be gone in a matter of weeks. Besides, Janet had witnessed the disaster he'd made of his marriage.

He was also surprised that Janet had pushed for this dinner party. When he'd ordered the knockout dress, he'd never expected that Holly would actually parade around in it here at Jabiru Creek. He'd only ever imagined her wearing it when she was back in America.

He could easily picture her at a cocktail party—somewhere flash with marble floors and fountains and a string quartet playing beneath potted palms. She'd sip a Martini and converse with some handsome Ivy League guy about Tolstoy and Beethoven and quantum physics.

But, if Gray was honest, he should admit that deep down he also hoped that wearing the dress would prompt Holly to remember him. And his kids, of course. And the time she'd spent here.

Would she miss them as much as they were going to miss her?

Hell. Alarmed by how suddenly downbeat he felt, Gray hurried through to his bathroom to shave with extra care.

'Wow, you look awesome, Daddy!'

Anna was the first to greet Gray when he arrived in the kitchen, dressed and ready for dinner.

'You look pretty swish, too,' he said, as his daughter performed a pirouette in her green plaid party dress. 'And so do you, Josh.'

Josh, in jeans and a button-down shirt, was more interested in playing with the puppies.

Janet was busy at the stove and she was wearing an apron over her best black dress and turquoise beads, and

Ted was there, too, standing in the corner, looking scrubbed and smart with his damp hair carefully combed over his bald patch.

'Don't you get paw marks on your shirt,' Janet told Josh, then she let her eyes run over Gray and gave him a nod of approval.

'Thanks for ironing these,' he said.

'I didn't want you slinging a tie on over a crumpled old work shirt and jeans.'

He grinned. 'You know me too well.' Taking a step towards the stove, he sniffed. 'Dinner smells great. What is it? Roast beef?'

'Roast rib of beef with Yorkshire pudding.'

'And your special gravy and horseradish sauce?'

'Of course.'

'Fantastic. I could eat a horse and chase the rider.'

'Daddy!' cried Anna, shocked.

Gray laughed and tickled her tummy. 'Where's Holly?'

'Still getting ready.' His daughter pulled a face. 'She's been getting ready for hours an' hours.'

'Maybe she wants to make a grand entry,' suggested Janet.

Gray shook his head. 'That's not Holly's style.'

Janet turned from the stove. 'Well…everything's more or less ready here. Why don't you pop along to Holly's room to let her know?'

Something like a bolt of lightning ripped through Gray. Going to Holly's bedroom was not a great idea, not with all the fantasies he fought off on a daily basis. He almost suggested that Anna should go to fetch Holly, but then…

His curiosity overpowered him. He was dead anxious to see her all dressed up.

Ridiculously, his throat was dry and his palms clammy

as he walked down the hallway and tapped on her door. 'Dinner's almost ready,' he called.

The door opened and Holly peeped out, and the top half of her, which was all Gray could see, looked amazingly beautiful. Holly was always pretty, but tonight she'd done something special with her hair, and with her make-up.

He'd never dreamed that eye shadow and mascara and lipstick could make such a dramatic difference. Combined with the dress, the whole effect was breathtaking.

'Wow,' he whispered.

Holly rolled her eyes. 'But, Houston, we have a problem.'

'A problem?' What on earth could it be?

Of course, he'd still only seen the top half of her, but she looked sensational. 'Is there something wrong with the dress?'

Holly shook her head. 'The dress is perfect. *However*—' She gave a sheepish smile as she opened the door fully. 'Ta-da!'

The dress *was* perfect. Holly was perfect. She looked like a princess, a movie star, a fashion model. Except...

Gray's eyes travelled down to her feet.

'Not a good look, is it?' she said with an embarrassed smile.

She was wearing sneakers.

'I didn't bring anything with heels, Gray. I was coming to the Outback, you know, so I brought sneakers and walking boots.'

He felt an urge to laugh, but Holly looked as if she might tip either way—into hysterical laughter or into tears.

'It's my fault,' he said quickly. 'I should have thought to order glass slippers.'

And then, because it was the most natural thing in the world to do, he opened his arms to her.

Her hair was silky and fragrant, her skin deliciously scented, and her body felt sensational beneath the soft fabric of the dress. In a New York second, Gray was overwhelmed with the need he'd been battling since their night together.

Unfortunately, what he had in mind would almost certainly mess up Holly's perfect make-up. Her lipstick and mascara would end up all over his shirt. And then…for sure, his shirt and her dress would have to go…and…

And he dropped his hands before he weakened.

'I think these shoes are perfect for tonight,' he murmured against her ear. 'Everyone's going to love how you look.'

Perhaps it was best that Holly wasn't wearing high heels. Gray's lovely embrace had thrown her completely off balance and her legs were dangerously wobbly as they went down the hallway to the kitchen.

He'd awoken every memory of their one night together—the scent of his skin, the hardness of his body, the daring intimacy of his touch and the incredible fireworks.

Fortunately, by the time they joined the others, she'd taken enough deep, slow breaths that she was calmer. More or less.

And the sneakers provided a welcome distraction. They were greeted by smiles of sympathy, and everyone was gratifyingly complimentary about the dress. Holly was truly made to feel like the guest of honour.

The meal was superb. Holly had never eaten golden, sumptuous Yorkshire pudding with roast beef. It was delicious, and it was such fun for everyone to be all dressed up and to eat in the dining room. They were in high spirits and, even though the conversation was mostly about puppies, or the horse-riding lessons the children were about to begin, no one minded. Best of all, Holly's feet were hidden under the table for most of the evening.

Throughout the meal she was super-aware of Gray. Their glances kept colliding and, each time, tingles broke out on her skin. The warmth in his eyes seemed to suggest that he was remembering all the things they were supposed to be forgetting.

Every time she caught him looking at her, her body would flash and she'd remember the thrill of his arms wrapped around her and the seductive scent of his after-shave, his powerful body burning against hers.

It was something of a relief, at the end of the meal, to jump up and help Janet to clear the table.

Of course, Janet tried to protest. 'You don't have to help, Holly.'

'I do. You've been slaving all day, and I'm very grateful. But now I'm going to wash up while Gray tells the children a bedtime story. No arguments, please, Janet. You go off and put your feet up and read your new magazine.'

Holly didn't check to see how Gray felt about this arrangement. This evening, she didn't want to be involved in helping him with the children. She was happy to stay in the kitchen. Really. It was a matter of self-preservation.

'You're a living treasure,' Janet told her fondly. 'I must admit my bunions are killing me. But at least put an apron on.' She unhooked a long white wraparound apron from the back of the kitchen door.

Holly was still wearing this when Gray came back into the kitchen half an hour later, just as she finished scouring the last baking dish.

Of course she looked totally unglamorous now, wrapped in the voluminous apron, with her hands in rubber gloves, her bare ankles showing and her feet in sneakers. But perhaps it was just as well, she thought. She'd had a lovely evening, and the dress had been fabulously exciting, but it was time to come back to earth.

Gray had taken off his tie and loosened his shirt collar, but nothing could dim his gorgeousness.

'You really are Cinderella tonight,' he said. 'Home from the ball and straight into the kitchen.'

Holly snapped off the rubber gloves and smiled. 'I don't mind. It's the least I could do after Janet cooked such a fabulous meal. That roast was so tasty and the lemon syllabub was divine.'

Reaching behind her, she untied the apron strings, but she felt strangely self-conscious. With the red dress about to be revealed once more, and Gray's intense gaze fixed on her, removing the apron felt as risqué as a striptease.

She concentrated on *not* blushing as she hung the apron on its hook behind the door.

'I think that dress might be the wisest purchase I've ever made,' Gray said, watching her from behind.

Holly concentrated harder on remaining calm. 'It really was very kind of you to buy me something so beautiful.' Slowly she turned around, only to find his blue eyes watching her with heartbreaking attention.

She dropped her gaze to her sneakers. Surely they would sober her.

Gray said, 'You're the one who's been kind, Holly. You've given up your summer holiday to help the children, and now you're helping me as well—'

'It hasn't felt like I've given up anything. I love Anna and Josh and—' Holly bit down on her lower lip before she said anything dangerous that she'd regret. 'And I've had so many wonderful new experiences.'

She looked down at her hands. It had been a stroke of luck that she'd brought red nail varnish with her, especially as the colour matched the dress perfectly. But now, in the homestead kitchen, the bright nails looked citified and out of place.

Forcing a laugh, she said, 'Listen to us. We're talking as if I'm leaving already, when I still have weeks to go.'

'Yes,' Gray said, but he made an uncomfortable throat clearing sound. 'That's something I wanted to speak to you about.'

Holly felt suddenly ill. Reaching behind her, she grabbed the edge of the sink for support. 'Do you want me to leave earlier?'

'No, no. No way. You're welcome to stay as long as you like.' He let out a heavy sigh. 'But it's time I sent off the ads for the new nanny, and I was hoping you could help me with the wording.'

'Oh, yes, of course.'

It was ridiculous to feel so abruptly miserable. She knew that Gray wasn't going to take one look at her in the red dress and suddenly change his mind about never wanting another wife.

Fortunately, he'd never know that, despite her protests that they mustn't get too close and that she had an all-important job to return to, she'd still foolishly fallen in love with him.

'Of course,' she said quickly. 'I'd be happy to help you work up an ad.'

She had to keep busy—busy and businesslike.

'When do you want to start? Now? Why don't we do it here in the kitchen? There's pen and paper right here in the dresser.'

Holly was gabbling, talking to fill in gaps. Gaps were dangerous—they left room for tears.

Without waiting to gauge Gray's reaction, she retrieved the pen and paper and sat down at the kitchen table.

Gray moved more slowly, taking his time to stroll around

the table and sit opposite her, leaning back in his chair, long legs stretched beneath the table.

Not wanting to see the expression in his eyes, Holly kept her gaze on the page and, when he was seated, she spoke in her most businesslike voice. 'Right. Let's see what you'll need. I imagine you'll want someone over eighteen years of age?'

When he didn't answer immediately, she shot him a sharp look. 'You want an adult to look after your children, don't you, Gray?'

'Yes,' he said, frowning and looking uncomfortable. 'Yes, sure.'

Holly began to make a list. 'And someone who enjoys and values working with children?'

Gray nodded.

She made another note. 'With a first aid certificate?'

'I...I guess that would be handy. Mostly, I want a good teacher.'

'You'd be unlikely to attract a person with teaching qualifications, but you should aim for someone who can provide stimulating activities for the children.'

'That's right.'

Oh, God. This was killing her. 'I'm sure you'd prefer someone who can produce a variety of age appropriate activities that encourage the development of life skills.'

Gray blinked. 'That sounds good.'

'And you'd want to be able to check this person's references.'

He nodded unhappily.

'What about public liability insurance?'

'We'd need to sort out something. I already have employee insurance.' Letting out a sigh, Gray reached for the salt and pepper shakers that had been left in the middle of the table and began to move them about like chess pieces.

Under the table, Holly squeezed her left fist tightly, letting her fingernails dig into her palm. The more it hurt, the better—anything to distract her from getting too emotional. 'I think this list covers the most important requirements,' she said. 'Can you think of anything else?'

'No.'

'If you tell me which newspapers you'd like to advertise in—'

'I'll get Ted to give you a list of them in the morning. And…er…I think there are sites on the Internet as well.'

'Yes, there are bound to be.'

'Ted will know.'

'Great.' Holly noted: *Internet—ask Ted.* And she pressed so hard she made a hole in the paper. She set the pen down and rubbed her arms. Now that this discussion was over, she felt a chill, as if she was coming down with something.

'I guess we won't bother with the reading tonight,' Gray said.

'That might be best.' Again, she kept her eyes on the page. 'It's been a big day. You could always read one of your new books in—' her cheeks burned '—in…bed.'

'Now that's a novel idea.'

Keep busy…

Holly rubbed at her eyes as if she were sleepy, but mostly she wanted to make sure there were no tears. Then she tore the page with her list from the notepad and got up to put the pad and pen away in the drawer. Behind her, she heard the scrape of Gray's chair on the timber floorboards.

She realised she was shaking from the effort of holding herself together. What an idiot she was. She couldn't fall apart now just because they'd drawn up an ad for her replacement. She'd always known this was going to happen. It was what she'd planned right from the start when Gray first asked her to help him out. How crazy to feel so upset. Anyone would think she'd just signed her own death warrant.

Turning back to the table, she reached for the list, but she still couldn't bring herself to look at Gray, even though he was now standing quite close to her.

She heard his heavy sigh, felt it reverberate all the way through her. What did he have to sigh about?

'I wish it could be you,' he said softly.

Holly froze.

'I know it's selfish,' he said, still in that same soft, low voice. 'But I wish we didn't have to find a new nanny.'

She allowed herself to look at him then. His eyes were extra-shiny and his mouth tight as if he, too, were holding his emotions in. He sent her a quarter smile and his shoulders lifted in a shrug. 'Where are we going to find another Holly?'

Her heartbeats thundered in her ears. Wild, extravagant hope lifted her like a high wind. She struggled to ignore it. 'I'm replaceable.'

'No, you're not.'

She gasped, had to grip the back of the chair. 'Are you saying that you want me to stay?'

'I know you can't stay. You're lined up for a fabulous new career.'

'But if you really needed me—'

His eyes widened. 'You'd stay?'

'I...I might.'

Had she really said that? Had she deliberately put herself out on a limb? Was she out of her mind?

Gray's throat worked. 'It would be perfect, wouldn't it? The kids love you. You're so good for them, Holly.' His words flowed freely enough, but he was standing to attention as if he were facing a court martial.

Holly waited for him to go on, waited for him to tell her that it wasn't only his children who needed her.

Please, please let him need me, too.

Perhaps now was the time to admit that she'd been falling steadily in love with him since she'd arrived at Jabiru. They could both admit that their night together and the closeness they'd shared on so many levels had grown into something deeper—something lasting and wonderful.

As they stood in the middle of the kitchen, Holly felt the Outback night close in around them. The only sound was the ticking of the old-fashioned clock on the wall beside the dresser. She could see the baking dishes on the drainer, shiny and silver after her conscientious scouring.

She saw Gray's hands clench and unclench. Remembered the way those strong hands had held her this evening, remembered the burning need she'd sensed in him.

Say something, Gray. I won't stay unless you want me, so just tell me the truth about how you feel. Let me off the hook, or reel me in, but don't leave me dangling.

When he didn't speak up, Holly knew she had to say something or scream.

'What about you?' Her voice sounded impossibly loud, bouncing off the walls. Then, in a more moderate tone, she asked, 'Do you want me to stay?'

CHAPTER ELEVEN

DO YOU want me to stay?

Gray bit back a groan of frustration. Of course he wanted Holly to stay, but how could he ask that of her?

It meant asking her to give up *everything*—her job, her home, her country. It meant asking her to commit to *his* lifestyle, *his* family, *his* country. And it meant taking their relationship to a whole new level, a committed level.

He'd vowed he'd never take that risk again.

Chelsea had quickly come to resent this place, just as his mother had. They'd been miserable here. He couldn't bear to make Holly unhappy.

Okay, it was true that she seemed to like the Outback. And if he'd been looking for a wife and had made a wish list of qualities he needed, Holly would score a tick in every box.

She was fun to be with. She fitted into Jabiru as if she'd been raised in the Outback. His kids adored her. Janet and Ted adored her.

And he owed her so much. She'd lifted such a burden from him, and she'd shown him that his future was not restricted by his past. But beyond all that she was so sweet and sexy and she was—*Holly*.

She'd wound her way around his heart. He wanted her— wanted her kisses, her warm sexy body. Tonight, seeing her in the red dress and keeping his distance had been torture.

His imagination kept playing scenes in his head of peeling the lovely red dress from her, slowly, slowly... And, as each inch of her soft, silky skin was revealed, he'd shower her with kisses until they were both almost blind with wanting, and then he would make love to her. Tenderly or passionately.

Her wish would be his command.

But he couldn't indulge his selfish fantasies. He had to be practical and clear-headed, had to remember that where women were concerned he'd fooled himself too many times. Holly was an educated city woman—like his mother and Chelsea. Eventually, her enjoyment of his isolated lifestyle would begin to pall and she'd long for her old life.

He had to be strong, and his task was painfully clear. He had no right to keep Holly here. He had to set her free. Now. Tonight. He had to send her back to the brilliant career and the secure future that awaited her in America.

Hands plunged in his pockets to stop himself from weakening and touching her, he gave her the only possible answer. 'I can't ask you to stay, Holly.'

Her head jerked up and she opened her mouth as if she was about to speak, but he held up his hand.

Now that he'd started, he had to get this out.

'I know my children are very important to you, and I know you'll miss them and they'll sure as anything miss you. But I'll do my best for them, Holly. You've shown us the way.'

He had to pause to swallow the brick that had wedged in his throat. 'I...I think we'll be okay from now on. We'll always be incredibly grateful to you.'

Holly's lips trembled and Gray felt his courage failing. 'You have a wonderful job to go back to,' he said quickly, before he changed his mind. 'A great life in America. You know I couldn't possibly ask you to give that up.'

She stood very still, not meeting his gaze, with her arms wrapped over her stomach as if she were nursing an ache.

'You have your wonderful family there, too,' he added. 'And I know how important your new job is. I've never seen anyone as excited as you were when you got that phone call at JFK. Your face lit up and you punched the air like you'd won a gold medal.'

Her eyes widened with surprise, as if he'd reminded her of something she'd forgotten.

'You need to go home, Holly.'

'You want me to go.' It was a statement rather than a question.

'I don't want you to be trapped here.'

Her intelligent gaze narrowed and for a moment he thought she was going to debate this final point, but then her mouth twisted into a grotesque attempt at a smile. She snatched up the piece of paper with the list she'd made for the ad, turned and almost ran from the room.

Gray watched her red dress and sneakers disappear and his heart was as heavy as a stone.

Holly reached her room without crying, but she was trembling all over. In all her life, she'd never felt so filled with despair. Worse, she wasn't even sure how she'd reached this point.

Until this evening, she hadn't realised how very badly she wanted to stay at Jabiru. Now she knew she wanted it so desperately she felt as if her happiness depended on staying here. But she could only stay if Gray felt as strongly about her as she felt about him. Tonight, he'd only talked about his children's needs.

Couldn't he guess she needed him?

She loved him.

Oh, help. That was the truth of it, although she had no idea when it had happened. Was it tonight when Gray had held her? Or at the point when she'd picked up the pen and paper to make the fateful list? Or had it started at the gorge?

Perhaps she'd been changing from the moment Gray had walked into the apartment in New York?

Oh, God, why hadn't she been more careful? She'd known all along that Gray would never risk a second marriage—especially to another American—and if he'd asked her to stay he would have felt obliged to marry her.

How could she let this happen to her again—this cruel, unbearable pain? This cold ache in her heart was so much worse than after the break-up with Brandon. When she left Jabiru she would leave part of her soul behind.

It was ages before she rose from the bed and super, super-carefully took off the lovely red dress and hung it back on its hanger. Then she changed into her pyjamas and went through to the bathroom to take off her make-up, telling herself that the routine would help.

It didn't.

When she climbed into bed and opened the book on her nightstand, she knew she had no hope of reading herself to sleep. She lay there, replaying every painful word of the night's terrible conversation.

When she finally turned out the lamp, she buried her face in her pillow and let her tears fall…

'You're so comfortable and capable with your children now,' Holly told Gray several evenings later. 'Those riding lessons have made such a difference. They're proper little

Outback kids now and you're going to manage just fine on your own.'

'I don't think I'm ready to fly solo yet.'

'Of course you are,' she said with necessary briskness. 'You've made great strides with the reading, and it's just a matter of practice now. You should read to Anna and Josh. They'll love it.'

The suggestion seemed to please him and he grinned, looking unbearably cute, like Josh. 'I have to admit I feel as if a huge burden has rolled off my shoulders.'

'I'm glad.' Ignoring the sudden nervous tumble in her stomach, she said, 'Actually, as things have turned out, you'll have to manage on your own quite soon.'

Gray frowned. 'How have things turned out? What do you mean?'

'I've had an email from the principal at my new school and she'd like me to start work earlier than we'd originally planned.'

He stared at her, shocked. Then his blue eyes narrowed suspiciously, as if he sensed something wasn't quite right about her claim.

The tumbling in Holly's stomach intensified. Could Gray guess that she'd engineered this new development?

She'd felt so despairing and heartbroken that she'd had to do something. Staying at Jabiru Creek had become the worst form of self-torture. Each bird call, each sunset, each family meal, each evening session alone with Gray reminded her of everything she was losing. In desperation, she'd written to the principal, advising that she was available to start sooner, if it suited them.

'What's the rush?' Gray asked, so quietly Holly could only just hear him.

'A benefactor has died and left a large sum of money to the school library, so they'd like me to start early, buying in new books for the new school year.' She flashed a falsely bright smile. 'A spending spree. Lucky me.'

He sank back in his chair, his expression gratifyingly sombre, but Holly no longer fooled herself that his gloominess was of any special significance. Her early departure would be an inconvenience, but Gray would manage. Anna and Josh would manage, too. They had a father who loved them, who would do anything for them.

The advertisement for the new nanny had been sent to several newspapers and Internet sites, so that ball was rolling. Until the nanny arrived, Janet could be taught how to set up the School of the Air each morning and the teacher would take it from there. Meanwhile, for Holly, leaving early had become an increasing necessity, a sanity saver.

'When do you have to leave here?'

'I thought I'd get a lift on the next mail plane.'

Shock flared in Gray's eyes. 'But that's only three days away.'

'Yes.'

He launched to his feet, ploughed a frantic hand through his hair. 'What about the children? They'll get such a shock.'

'Not really. They've known all along that I was eventually leaving and I've already been preparing them for their new nanny.'

He came to an abrupt halt with his hands sunk in his pockets, his cheeks leached of colour. 'They'll still be shocked. When will you tell them?'

'I was hoping we could both tell them together, tomorrow morning.'

This was met by stormy silence.

'You'll do that, won't you, Gray? You'll back me up?'

It was ages before he answered. But, to her relief, he finally nodded, said very quietly, 'Yes, of course.'

* * *

The only good thing about the next three days was that they were incredibly busy. Suddenly there was so much for Holly to organise—flights home, a hotel booking in Sydney, detailed notes for the new nanny and farewell emails to all the Outback mothers, teachers and governesses she'd met via School of the Air.

She spent as much time as she could with Anna and Josh, and of course there were weepy moments and lots of questions and reassuring hugs.

'You'll come back to us, won't you?'

Holly couldn't answer this. 'I'll see you when your daddy brings you to America to your grandma and grandpa,' she said instead.

She set them up with email accounts, so they could write to her when she was back in the US.

There were no more reading lessons with Gray. The evenings were taken up with farewell activities. Janet insisted on a party and she invited everyone on the property, including the ringers. Holly really liked these easy-going, laconic men and partying with them reminded her of how much she was going to miss their dry jokes and colourful stories about mustering and droving.

On the last night Gray made a campfire down on the riverbank and he roasted freshwater crayfish that he'd caught in the river that afternoon. They ate out under the stars and the food was delicious, the evening magical. The children danced their own version of an Aboriginal corroboree around the fire and Gray told another Hector Owl story. Holly had no idea how she held back the tears.

The actual farewell the next morning was the worst moment, of course. No one—not even Gray—could pretend to be cheerful, and down at the airstrip, the children clung to Holly, tears flowing.

'I love you, Holly,' Josh whispered.

'I love you, too, darling.'

Anna cried. 'I don't want you to go.'

'I know, but you have Daddy now, honey. And you re-member what we said? You're going to be brave, aren't you?'

Holly was sure she could actually feel her heart break-ing. These gorgeous children had lost their mother and now they were losing her. She wasn't going to be like her own mom who'd married a lonely widower to become his cherished wife and his children's dearly loved stepmom.

She was flying out of their lives.

Janet was too grim-lipped to speak. She gave Holly a fierce, silent hug.

But it was the bleak look in Gray's eyes that almost burst Holly's floodgates.

'All the best with the new job,' he said gruffly, hug-ging her close so that she felt his heart thundering before he stepped quickly away. 'I hope that school knows how lucky they are to have you.'

By a minor miracle Holly managed not to cry, but the worst was yet to come—climbing into the tiny plane and taking off, watching the homestead and the outhouses and the tiny figures beside the airstrip growing smaller and smaller until they were no more than dots…

The pilot sent her a sympathetic smile. 'You'll be back,' he said.

Holly shook her head. She would write emails and letters and make phone calls to Anna and Josh, and she would see them whenever they came to the States, but she wouldn't come back to Jabiru Creek.

She couldn't bear to be received as a visitor, an outsider, in the place where she'd left a huge chunk of her heart.

* * *

They were asleep at last.

Gray held his breath as he closed the story book and backed out of the children's room.

Contrary to Holly's predictions, Anna and Josh had reacted rather badly to her departure and he expected them to wake again at any moment. For now, thank heavens, they were sleeping like baby angels.

He tiptoed down the hall to his study, steeling himself for the empty space on the sofa. Even so, Holly's absence hit him like an icepick in the chest.

He'd done the right thing by letting her go, but he couldn't believe that doing the right thing could feel so bottom-of-the-pit bad.

How amazing that one girl had made such a difference in the lives of all of them here. Everyone at Jabiru loved Holly. They'd all been cheered by her sunshiny personality. They'd respected her knowledge and skills, and they'd appreciated her genuine interest and desire to help. With her latest book-swapping scheme, she'd even begun spreading the goodwill further to women in outlying properties.

Gray didn't dare—or, rather, couldn't bear to list his private reasons for missing Holly.

He *might* have felt better about waving her off if he'd been confident that she was happy to go. But that was the killer, the worry eating away at him now like a worm in an apple—Holly had been a different girl these past few days.

She'd put on a brave face, smiling her way through all the farewell activities but, although she'd laughed and said how wonderful it all was to have so many great memories to take home, Gray had been watching her closely and he'd seen her frightening fragility. He'd seen the tremble in her smile and the new cautiousness, as if she was scared she might crack like an eggshell unless she was very, very careful.

He'd been so sure he was doing the right thing in sending her away, but now he felt sick and uncertain. And bloody lonely.

'You're a sight for sore eyes,' Janet remarked the next morning when Gray came into the kitchen, yawning.

'Anna had a nightmare last night,' he said, rubbing a hand over his unshaven jaw. 'I took her in to sleep with me, and then I couldn't get back to sleep.'

Janet paused in the process of stirring scrambled eggs. 'That's the first nightmare Anna's had for ages, isn't it?'

He nodded as he poured himself a mug of tea.

'Gray, you know what's caused it, don't you?'

'I guess she might be missing Holly.'

His housekeeper shot him a look that made it clear she considered him one sandwich short of a picnic. 'Of course the poor little lamb is missing Holly.' Turning the gas beneath the saucepan down, Janet came over to him and lowered her voice. 'Where are the children now?'

'They're still getting dressed. They slept in. Why?'

'I've got something to say to you. Unfortunately, I had to wait till Holly was gone before I thought you'd be ready to listen.'

His housekeeper studied him, and then she nodded smugly. 'You're in a bad way, aren't you? Can't sleep, face like a dropped meat pie.'

He began to make excuses. 'But Holly was—'

'You've realised you made a big mistake, letting Holly go.'

Gray almost denied this, but what was the point? 'I had to.'

'Forgive me for saying this, Gray, but that's rubbish.

That wonderful girl loved living here, and she was perfect for Jabiru in every way. If you think she's cut from the same cloth as your former wife, then you're thicker than two short planks.' Janet leaned closer. 'And the really terrible thing is Holly *loves* you, Gray. You must know she's mad about you. She loves all of us, bless her tender heart. She loves this place. But even a blind man could see how she feels about you.'

The kitchen swam before Gray. His throat stung. 'But her job—'

'Do you really think Holly would care two hoots for that job if she thought she could be here with you?'

He had to set his mug of tea down before it slipped from his shaking fingers.

'Have I been a coward, Janet?'

'Lord love you, no. You're just a man, after all.' Picking up a corner of her apron, Janet dabbed at her eyes. 'And I understand you're scared you'll be hurt again.'

'I'm not, actually. Not with Holly. It's *her* happiness I'm worried about.'

'Then you should stop worrying right now and do something about it. If you let Holly get all the way back to America, I might never forgive you.'

'But she's already on her way home.'

Janet shook her head. 'She has a two-night stopover in Sydney. Thought she might as well see a little more of Australia before she leaves.'

'Two nights.' Gray's heart swooped high, then took a dive. 'But she only has one night left. How the hell can I get to Sydney by tonight?'

Janet smiled and patted his cheek. 'Where there's a will there's nearly always a way.'

* * *

Sydney was a beautiful city. Holly woke to a sunny and dazzling winter's day—and where better to spend it than out on the Harbour?

She walked to Circular Quay and took a ferry ride, cruising beneath the famous coat-hanger bridge and past the dramatic sails of the Opera House, stopping at a five star seafood restaurant right on the sparkling waterfront.

She tried to enjoy herself. Honestly. But it wasn't easy to have fun when her senses were completely numb.

This stopover in Sydney was so different from last time, when she'd first arrived here with Gray and the children, all excited about their new adventure. It felt like a lifetime ago. Was it really only a month?

In the evening, she forced herself to go out again. She'd bought a pair of snappy high heels to wear with the red dress. Why waste it?

After a toss-up between a musical, a play or a movie, she opted for the play because one of her favourite actresses was in the leading role. It was rather embarrassing, though. She cried rather noisy buckets in the third act—which was all very tragic—and people around her stared.

She managed a little make-up repair in the Ladies room and then treated herself to coffee and dessert at a trendy little wine bar. Normally, a chocolate soufflé would lift her spirits, no matter how low they'd been.

Not tonight.

Gray paced the hallway outside Holly's hotel room, his stomach bunching with nerves. It was past eleven and she still wasn't back. How much longer could he wait before he was accused by a hotel employee of stalking?

Everything had been going his way until now. It was quite amazing the way fate had smiled on him this morning when he'd rung an old mate, a charter pilot, on the off chance. Luckily, Jack had been willing to juggle schedules just to get Gray to Sydney on time, and Janet had been able to tell him where Holly was staying.

The only spanner in the works was Holly, who was clearly spending a night on the town.

Gray patted his jacket pocket and felt for the small rectangular envelope, and the knots in his stomach pulled tighter than fencing wire. A hard lump filled his throat. Could he do this?

He'd left messages on Holly's phone, but if she got back very late there was every chance that she wouldn't bother to check them.

Could he follow through with his alternative? Could he risk the pain that had haunted him all his life and leave this note under her door?

Memories crowded in—awful, sickening memories of the one other time he'd tried such a desperate measure—his plea to his mother to stop her from leaving Jabiru.

The stress of repeating history brought him out in a cold sweat. This time he had everything to lose.

And everything to gain.

His hand was shaking as he took the envelope from his pocket. It was such a small piece of paper, so few words. Such a simple task to slide the note through the narrow crack below the door. Such a small window of opportunity in which to convince Holly.

As he knelt in the empty hallway, his mind flashed an image of a heartbroken boy, trembling with hope as he slipped a note beneath his mother's door.

Was he mad to try this again?

After her coffee and dessert, Holly wandered back to her hotel but she felt lonelier than ever. The streets were *full* of couples—couples holding hands and laughing, couples with their arms around each other, couples kissing in shadowy doorways.

It was a relief to reach her hotel. The girl at the front desk sent her a smile when she came in, but Holly thought she saw sympathy in the girl's eyes, as if she was sorry for her—all dressed up and on her own. She hurried into the elevator and whizzed up to the nineteenth floor.

As the elevator doors opened and she stepped out into the carpeted hallway, she saw her reflection in a gilt-edged mirror hanging above an elaborate flower arrangement.

Her red dress looked as gorgeous as ever. In fact it looked even better now—she'd lost weight in the last week and she'd acquired cheekbones and a tragic air. Like a heroine in a sad love story.

Ha, ha. Not funny.

She continued down the hall to her room, slotted the key in the lock, heard its click and the door swung silently open. So much for her last night in Australia.

CHAPTER TWELVE

THERE was a white envelope lying on the carpet just inside the door. Holly saw it, but she knew it would be her bill and she was too weary and despondent to worry about it now. Stepping over it, she told herself she would deal with it first thing in the morning when she checked out.

She went through to the luxurious bathroom with its gorgeous plunge bath and gold taps and rows of pretty little bottles. A warm bath with fragrant oils might help her to sleep.

Sitting on the edge of the bath, she started the water running and unscrewed the lid on one of the bottles. She poured the liquid, inhaling the scents of jasmine and rose but, as she watched it swirl then foam and turn into bubbles, something tugged at a corner of her mind.

Something about that white envelope—

Perhaps she should take another look at it.

Leaving the bath running, she went back to the little entrance hallway. Her name was on the front of the envelope and it was handwritten, or rather printed in an unskilled hand. Picking it up, she felt a nervous flurry in her chest. Then shivers ran down her arms.

Her heart began to race.

Stop it. Calm down.

It wasn't a hotel bill. It was the last thing Holly had

expected—something she'd never thought she'd see in this lifetime—a note handwritten in familiar shaky printing. Her legs were so weak she had to lean against the wall as she read it.

The message was perfectly simple.

Please stay. I love you. G xxxxxxxx.

A sob broke from her and her hand flew to her mouth. Her vision blurred and her heart pounded like a marching band.

She could scarcely see the note for her tears. Her mind was a whirlpool of disconnected thoughts. How had the note got here? Where was Gray?

But, before she could begin to think about answers to these questions, she heard an ominous trickling sound. *Oh, God.* The bathwater was overflowing.

As she dashed into the bathroom to turn off the taps, the phone beside her bed began to ring.

'I'm sorry, sir. There's still no answer from Room 1910.'

Gray muttered his curt thanks and prowled back to his post on the far side of the hotel lobby. It was close to midnight now and he wasn't sure how much longer he should pace the hotel's marble floors.

Once or twice he had ducked outside to stroll along Castlereagh Street for a breath of fresh air, but he'd always checked back with the concierge desk on his return. He was sure he hadn't missed Holly, and this last call to her room had still brought no answer.

Where was she? He was fast losing hope.

Tired of pacing, he sank into the leather armchair and thought about ordering another coffee. But he'd consumed so much caffeine tonight, his eyes would soon be out on stalks.

'Sir?'

A voice at Gray's elbow brought him leaping to his feet.

The uniformed concierge, a man of around fifty with a florid face, smiled. 'Mr Kidman?'

Gray's heart thudded. 'Yes.'

'Miss O'Mara has returned. She telephoned the desk and left a message for you.' He handed Gray a folded piece of paper.

Gray opened it, and died a thousand deaths.

It was a handwritten note, not printed, but written in a spiky script with curls and flourishes disfiguring the familiar shape of the letters. He hadn't a hope of deciphering it.

Already the concierge was returning to his desk. Gray hurried after him.

'Excuse me.'

The man turned, eyebrows raised. 'Can I help, sir?'

Gray's face burned crimson. His throat closed over and he wanted to turn and run for the hills. In the past he would have found any excuse to avoid this embarrassment. He would have given up and walked away rather than expose his shame.

Now, his hand shook as he held out the note. 'Would you—' he began, but his voice was hoarse and choked. He tried again. 'Would you mind telling me what this note says?'

The concierge covered his surprise quite creditably once he got over his initial jaw-drop.

'Of course, sir,' he said super-politely. 'Perhaps I should

apologise for my handwriting.' He cleared his throat. 'The note says: *Sorry I missed your calls. I'm in my room now. Please come up.*'

Holly was waiting by the door, and she opened it at the first knock.

Gray was dressed in a dark jacket and tie, and he looked more heartbreakingly handsome than ever. She wanted to hurl herself into his arms; she'd been bursting with excitement since she'd read his note.

But she didn't move. She was worried that she might have somehow misread his message—although how could you misinterpret *I love you?* There was always the chance that it didn't mean quite what she'd instantly hoped. Tonight she couldn't risk taking anything for granted.

'I know it's late,' Gray said. 'But I had to see you.'

Despite her wildly thumping heart, she tried to speak calmly. 'I've been out. I went to a play.'

'How was it?' He looked and sounded as nervous as she felt, probably because he could see how red and swollen her eyes and nose were.

'The play was fabulous.' She waggled her fingers at her puffy face. 'Sorry about this damp look. I'm okay, really. Just being a girl, as my brothers would say.'

He looked worried. 'It must have been a sad play.'

'Yes, it was a tragedy.'

'Can I come in, Holly?'

'Oh, yes, of course. Sorry.'

Dizzy with excitement and fear, she led him down the little hallway that opened into her room which was dominated by a very large king-size bed.

There was only one chair, a pretty pink upholstered armchair in the corner beside a standard lamp.

'You take that,' she said, pointing to it and feeling

uncomfortably like a movie director trying to direct a scene without having first read the script. 'I can sit on the bed.'

'I'd rather not sit.' Gray's wide shoulders and height seemed to take up a great deal of space in the middle of the room. His blue eyes shimmered. 'You got my note, didn't you?'

'Yes, it was such a surprise.' *Understatement of the century.*

'I kept it brief. Less risk of getting the spelling wrong.'

'I thought it was very brave of you,' she said, knowing what it must have cost Gray to repeat an action that held so many sad memories.

He shook his head. 'I shouldn't have left it so late.'

'Well, no, you shouldn't. It's after midnight.'

He reached for her hands and her whole body flamed at his touch. 'I should have spoken up before you left. I should have thrown myself in front of the plane.'

'Maybe I should have been brave enough to tell you I didn't want to go.'

He smiled. 'Really?'

'Of course. Leaving Jabiru was the hardest thing I've ever done.'

'I was so worried that I'd trap you if I asked you to stay.'

'I know. You're worried because of Chelsea.'

'I always felt as if I failed her. Our feelings for each other weren't enough to bridge the huge gaps between us. I didn't want to fail you, too, Holly.' He gave her hands a gentle squeeze. 'But you've taught me something important—to stop dwelling on the failures of my past.'

Looking down at her hands, he rubbed the backs of her knuckles with his thumbs. 'I was fooling myself when I said the kids and I could manage without you.' He smiled crookedly. 'We tried. We tried playing with the puppets, we tried reading stories and lighting a campfire down by the river. But none of it was any fun without you, Holly.'

She was starting to feel giddy with relief.

'There's so much about you that I've missed,' he murmured, reaching out and tracing her cheek with his thumb.

A tremor of happiness ran over her skin.

Gray smiled, then he let his hand drop and he was looking serious once more. 'But we need to talk about this job of yours. I know how much your career means to you and—'

Holly silenced him with a shake of her head. 'The job is just—a job, Gray. When I applied for it, there were at least sixty other people after it.'

'Which means?'

'Which means that one of those sixty can have it.' She smiled into his eyes. In the lamplight they were as blue and bright as the skies above his home. 'I'm a farm girl from Vermont, remember. I love your Outback and, better still—I grew up in a patchwork family.'

'So you did. I'd forgotten that.'

'The only job I really want is the one I left behind at Jabiru.'

Gray laughed, then he gathered her in for the most tender and gorgeous and earth-shattering kiss of her life. She never wanted it to end.

When he finally released her, he said, 'There's still one really important thing that I haven't told you.'

'What's that?'

As if he couldn't bear to not be touching her, Gray picked up her hands again and began playing with her fingers. 'The thing is that now, thanks to you, I know how to study and get new skills and a different job.'

'Why would you want a different job?'

'I would if you wanted me to.' He lifted her hands to his lips and began, very gently, to kiss her fingers. 'If it made you happier, I'd study, take a course. If you wanted to live in New York I'd learn how to be a fireman—whatever.'

'Wow. A New York fireman. Now, that's a tempting option.' To Holly's surprise, Gray didn't show the slightest double take, and that was when she knew for sure that they were going to be all right. His willingness to walk away from the security of Jabiru Creek Station was a bigger gesture than any avowal of love, written or spoken.

'I happen to be in love with you exactly the way you are,' she assured him. 'But I'm very honoured that you'd be willing to change your life for me.'

'I want us to be together for a very long time.'

'That happens to be my personal fantasy.'

She smiled again, letting the brilliance of her happiness show. Then, lifting her face, she brushed her lips over his. 'I'm a girl with simple needs. Truth be told, *this* is what makes me happy.'

With another brush of her lips, their kiss became even more spectacular and glorious than the last one.

Then, with one arm around Holly's shoulders and another beneath her knees, Gray scooped her into his arms.

'Wow,' he breathed.

'I know. I'm heavy. Sorry.'

He laughed. 'Not that. I've just noticed your fabulous new shoes.'

'Oh, yes.' Floating with happiness, Holly lifted her legs high, in a move that might have impressed dancers at the Moulin Rouge. Now they could both admire her slender black patent shoes with pointy toes and follow-me-home heels.

'I'm glad you like them,' she said. 'I think they go really

well with this lovely dress, and they're a definite improvement on the sneakers.'

'They're very elegant,' he murmured sexily in her ear. 'But I love you in sneakers. I might have to ask you to wear them for our wedding. What do you reckon?'

She grinned at him, more gloriously happy than she'd ever thought possible. 'If we're married out at your beautiful gorge, I might need sneakers.'

Gray smiled into her eyes. 'That sounds like a plan.'

'An absolutely perfect plan,' Holly agreed.

MAY 2011
HARDBACK TITLES

ROMANCE

Too Proud to be Bought	Sharon Kendrick
A Dark Sicilian Secret	Jane Porter
Prince of Scandal	Annie West
The Beautiful Widow	Helen Brooks
Strangers in the Desert	Lynn Raye Harris
The Ultimate Risk	Chantelle Shaw
Sins of the Past	Elizabeth Power
A Night With Consequences	Margaret Mayo
Cupcakes and Killer Heels	Heidi Rice
Sex, Gossip and Rock & Roll	Nicola Marsh
Riches to Rags Bride	Myrna Mackenzie
Rancher's Twins: Mum Needed	Barbara Hannay
The Baby Project	Susan Meier
Second Chance Baby	Susan Meier
The Love Lottery	Shirley Jump
Her Moment in the Spotlight	Nina Harrington
Her Little Secret	Carol Marinelli
The Doctor's Damsel in Distress	Janice Lynn

HISTORICAL

Lady Drusilla's Road to Ruin	Christine Merrill
Glory and the Rake	Deborah Simmons
To Marry a Matchmaker	Michelle Styles
The Mercenary's Bride	Terri Brisbin

MEDICAL™

The Taming of Dr Alex Draycott	Joanna Neil
The Man Behind the Badge	Sharon Archer
St Piran's: Tiny Miracle Twins	Maggie Kingsley
Maverick in the ER	Jessica Matthews

04011 Gen Std LP

 MILLS & BOON

MAY 2011
LARGE PRINT TITLES

ROMANCE

Hidden Mistress, Public Wife	Emma Darcy
Jordan St Claire: Dark and Dangerous	Carole Mortimer
The Forbidden Innocent	Sharon Kendrick
Bound to the Greek	Kate Hewitt
Wealthy Australian, Secret Son	Margaret Way
A Winter Proposal	Lucy Gordon
His Diamond Bride	Lucy Gordon
Juggling Briefcase & Baby	Jessica Hart

HISTORICAL

Courting Miss Vallois	Gail Whitiker
Reprobate Lord, Runaway Lady	Isabelle Goddard
The Bride Wore Scandal	Helen Dickson
Chivalrous Captain, Rebel Mistress	Diane Gaston

MEDICAL™

Dr Zinetti's Snowkissed Bride	Sarah Morgan
The Christmas Baby Bump	Lynne Marshall
Christmas in Bluebell Cove	Abigail Gordon
The Village Nurse's Happy-Ever-After	Abigail Gordon
The Most Magical Gift of All	Fiona Lowe
Christmas Miracle: A Family	Dianne Drake

JUNE 2011
HARDBACK TITLES

ROMANCE

Passion and the Prince	Penny Jordan
For Duty's Sake	Lucy Monroe
Alessandro's Prize	Helen Bianchin
Mr and Mischief	Kate Hewitt
Wife in the Shadows	Sara Craven
The Brooding Stranger	Maggie Cox
An Inconvenient Obsession	Natasha Tate
The Girl He Never Noticed	Lindsay Armstrong
The Privileged and the Damned	Kimberly Lang
The Big Bad Boss	Susan Stephens
Her Desert Prince	Rebecca Winters
A Family for the Rugged Rancher	Donna Alward
The Boss's Surprise Son	Teresa Carpenter
Soldier on Her Doorstep	Soraya Lane
Ordinary Girl in a Tiara	Jessica Hart
Tempted by Trouble	Liz Fielding
Flirting with the Society Doctor	Janice Lynn
When One Night Isn't Enough	Wendy S Marcus

HISTORICAL

Ravished by the Rake	Louise Allen
The Rake of Hollowhurst Castle	Elizabeth Beacon
Bought for the Harem	Anne Herries
Slave Princess	Juliet Landon

MEDICAL™

Melting the Argentine Doctor's Heart	Meredith Webber
Small Town Marriage Miracle	Jennifer Taylor
St Piran's: Prince on the Children's Ward	Sarah Morgan
Harry St Clair: Rogue or Doctor?	Fiona McArthur

05011 Gen Std LP

JUNE 2011
LARGE PRINT TITLES

ROMANCE

Flora's Defiance	Lynne Graham
The Reluctant Duke	Carole Mortimer
The Wedding Charade	Melanie Milburne
The Devil Wears Kolovsky	Carol Marinelli
The Nanny and the CEO	Rebecca Winters
Friends to Forever	Nikki Logan
Three Weddings and a Baby	Fiona Harper
The Last Summer of Being Single	Nina Harrington

HISTORICAL

Lady Arabella's Scandalous Marriage	Carole Mortimer
Dangerous Lord, Seductive Miss	Mary Brendan
Bound to the Barbarian	Carol Townend
The Shy Duchess	Amanda McCabe

MEDICAL™

St Piran's: The Wedding of The Year	Caroline Anderson
St Piran's: Rescuing Pregnant Cinderella	Carol Marinelli
A Christmas Knight	Kate Hardy
The Nurse Who Saved Christmas	Janice Lynn
The Midwife's Christmas Miracle	Jennifer Taylor
The Doctor's Society Sweetheart	Lucy Clark